About the author

Steve King was born in Old Coulsdon, within the London Borough of Croydon, but left the South of England at an early age. Very much now a Northerner, Steve has travelled the world extensively and lived abroad, choosing to put down roots in Barnoldswick, deep in Pendle Witch Country.

After leaving Oxford University, Steve had a successful business career, deciding to branch out from corporate life to pursue a portfolio of opportunities including writing, publishing and consultancy, balanced with an active need to be outdoors. A keen folk musician and Harley rider, Steve attempts to squeeze whatever he can from life and tries to live by the following adage:

> *Fear and pain are fleeting, regret and remorse everlasting. Carpe diem.*

Barlick Tales

Steve King

Bernulf
PUBLISHING

Bernulf Publishing Ltd
PO Box 51, Barnoldswick, BB18 9AB
Tel: 07527 003848
www.bernulf.com

First published in Great Britain by
Bernulf Publishing, 2009.
ISBN 978-0-9564215-0-0

Set in Agfa Rotis Serif 11/14pt.
Cover design and production by Sheldrick Rose Ltd.
www.sheldrickrose.co.uk

To my family and friends, who inspire, frustrate and tolerate me in equal quantities.

Part 1
The Midnight Rose

Chapter 1

'Mind if I sit here?' Jay looked up. It was late afternoon, sometime after four. He knew that because they had caught the 3:55 train from Leeds, getting them back in to Colne at around 5:30.

Jay was 11 years old. 11 years and one month to be precise, as he had celebrated his birthday in July, although 'celebrated' was not really the word to describe it. He was a strong boy, the type you would find hanging upside down from a tree on a Saturday afternoon or damming a stream. When he had half an hour to kill he could be found heading off across the fields with his friends.

The girl standing in the aisle was looking at the seat next to him. The carriage was surprisingly full for the time of day, particularly for a Thursday.

She looks harmless enough, he thought.

'Help yourself,' he said, moving his rucksack so that she could sit down. His rucksack went everywhere he did and carried all the essentials for a boy of his age. A Nintendo DS, a wallet with a variety of 'credit cards' (mostly expired store cards he had begged from his mother), diverse key rings and an assortment of toys that he had collected from McDonald's over the years. He placed the bag on the floor between his feet, being careful not to hit his mother's leg. She was sitting on the other side of the table and was fast asleep. He went back to looking at the magazine he had bought at Leeds station.

The girl sat quietly for some time before turning to Jay.

'Is that your mother?' she asked, pointing to the woman facing them across the table.

'Yes,' he said. 'Why do you ask?'

'No reason,' she said matter of factly. 'It's just that she looks like you.' The train rattled through a set of points before steadying itself for another straight portion of track. 'I guess that would be your sister then,' said the girl, carrying on the conversation that Jay thought had finished.

'That's right,' he said, 'and please don't tell me that I look like her as well. The day's been bad enough as it is.'

The girl smiled. 'I shall never understand why boys have such a hard time accepting that girls are no different to them, really. It seems that you all have some kind of anti-girl rules written down somewhere and hidden in a place that we can never find. My brother is exactly the same.'

Jay smiled. Not so much rules as a code of conduct he thought. He looked across at his sister, who was also asleep, and his smile ebbed away.

'Why so glum?' asked the girl as she watched Jay's expression change.

'Doesn't matter,' he said and he turned to look out of the window. This was more to hide the tear that was starting to roll down his cheek than it was to see where they had reached. He raised his hand and wiped his face. He had promised her he wouldn't cry.

'I'm going as far as Skipton,' declared the girl. 'Where are you heading for?'

'Same,' said Jay. 'We live in Barnoldswick.' He looked back at the girl, sure that she would not notice the slight reddening of his eyes.

'Why are you crying?' she asked. It was a simple question and asked in such a gentle way that instead of being annoyed Jay felt that he owed her an answer.

'My sister is sick,' he said quietly, not wanting to wake her or his mother.

'I'm sorry to hear that.'

Jay tried to smile. Somehow he felt that she really was sorry and not just saying it to be polite. For some reason he felt the urge to tell her more. He wasn't sure why. Maybe because he hadn't really talked to anyone about it or maybe because he knew he would not be seeing her again. People often say it is easier to talk to a stranger about problems.

Jay took a deep breath. 'She has cancer.'

There. He had said it. For the first time since the diagnosis he had been able to say those words. Somehow he felt better for it. Almost like a release of tension. 'She's been sick for a long time, but we only found out last month when the test results came back. Our local doctor had been saying it was mild anaemia for over a year and giving her iron tablets. I shall never forgive him.'

This was why he had not celebrated his birthday. How could he celebrate being 11 when he found out the same day that his sister was sick? So sick, in fact, that she was unlikely to reach 11 herself. He felt another tear welling up in his eye. 'We're just on our way back from St James' in Leeds where they've been doing more tests. That's why they're both so tired. My mother has hardly slept for a month and Chloe is always tired now. She seems to get weaker every day.'

He wasn't sure why he kept talking. It was almost as if he owed the girl an explanation. 'Leukaemia,' he said. 'Advanced leukaemia'. The girl looked at him for a moment.

'It can be a terrible strain,' she said.

This angered Jay. How could she say that? How could she know what a strain it was? His sister was sitting across from them dying and this girl was going to pretend that she knew what it was like. He steadied himself to let loose, but before he could open his mouth the girl spoke again.

'We lived through the same thing in my family,' she said, as if she was talking about the measles or chickenpox. 'My mother had to go through it alone because my father died when I was much younger.'

Jay stopped and looked at her. 'My father is also dead,' he said. 'He died three years ago in a car crash on the M65.'

'Never give up hope,' said the girl and she smiled again, looking out the window. 'Almost time for us to get off.'

She stood up and looked at Chloe who appeared incredibly peaceful, asleep with her head in her mother's lap. She looked pale, but otherwise healthy. The girl turned to look at Jay.

'Here,' she said, handing him a piece of paper. 'This might help. It certainly did for us,' and with that she turned and walked to the door as the train began to pull into Skipton.

Jay roused his mother and his sister from their deep – if fitfull – sleep, wanting to make sure they had enough time to get their things together before the train stopped at the station.

He glanced down at the piece of paper. On it was written a telephone number. 01282. That was the same code as his. He looked up again to see the girl disappearing behind other bodies as the train ground to a halt. For some reason she had a familiar look about her.

He had never found out her name, or where she came from, for that matter. He folded the piece of paper, opened his rucksack and pulled out his wallet. He carefully placed the telephone number in with his other important documents, slid the wallet back down inside the sack and pulled the tie cord tight again. Strange girl, he thought as he herded his family towards the carriage door. But then again, they all are.

Chloe managed a smile as Jay helped her down the aisle. He had become much more thoughtful in the last month. A shame it had taken something so dramatic to bring out the best in him, she thought to herself.

They made their way along the platform and out on to the main road. Jay looked this way and that to see if he could catch a glimpse of the girl.

Nothing. Their mother found a taxi and they all squeezed into the back of a very old and rather smelly Cavalier. It was a pity that they now needed to take a taxi home. The train had once stopped at Barnoldswick, but the line had been dismantled years ago. Where the tracks had been was now the domain of joggers, people walking their dogs and kids on bikes.

A shame really, thought Jay as they sat in the traffic jam trying to exit the town centre.

Chapter 2

Once back in the house, Kathy put the television on and helped Chloe get comfortable on the sofa. Although always outwardly cheerful, she was finding it hard to come to grips with the news about her daughter. In the last month she had read constantly about the symptoms, causes and possible cures for Chloe's condition.

She would never give up hope – ever. But she was also a realist. She had become that way after the death of her husband, Peter. Life had had to go on for her and the children and dwelling on the past would not help. Now she knew in her heart of hearts that Chloe was unlikely to recover, but she was certainly not going to let the children know that. She was busying herself in the kitchen getting tea ready when Jay walked in.

'Mum,' he said, 'when I was on the train, I got talking to a girl who came and sat with us. You were asleep. We talked about Chloe and she had been through the same thing in her family.'

'Poor girl,' said Kathy, secretly glad to hear that Jay was talking with someone, even if she was a complete stranger. 'What was her name?'

'I have no idea,' replied Jay. 'She got off in Skipton and I never had the chance to ask.' Jay told his mother about the piece of paper the girl had given him and he carefully took it out of his wallet and handed it to her. 'She said we should call the number. She said it might help us like it did her.'

Kathy looked at the number and smiled. 'That was very thoughtful of her,' she said looking at the paper but not really taking it in. She told Jay to go and wash up for tea. Without a further thought Kathy folded the paper and put it into the pocket of her apron.

With tea behind them and the summer skies still invitingly light, Jay and Chloe decided to go for a walk before bed. Kathy stayed to clean up the dishes while the children walked along Calf Hall Road and up the lane by the side of the disused cotton mill. This was perfect for Chloe as she loved to watch the beck, but she couldn't walk too far without getting very tired. Jay wondered if he should tell her about the girl on the train. Should he give her some vague hope based on a piece of paper handed to him by a total stranger? No, he thought, better not. Besides, his mother had obviously decided it was not worth following up on, judging by the way she had reacted when he had given it to her.

The sun was setting low and the beautiful reds and yellows seemed to dance in the sky as the wind gently blew across the meadow. The sheep moved slowly across to the children as soon as they arrived, curious to see what they might have brought with them. Sadly this time they were to be disappointed and quickly lost interest in them when an old man arrived on a quad bike with a bale of hay.

'Best be getting back,' said Jay, not wanting to keep her out too late in the cooling night air.

It was around nine when they got back to the house, just time for a bath and bed.

Chloe and Jay shared a bedroom in a two-up, two-down terraced house. They had moved there after their father had died. It was nice enough but Jay had often wished he had a little more privacy. However, now he was glad that he shared a room with Chloe because he would be close if she needed him.

Tonight was to be such a night.

He was woken at about midnight by Chloe

coughing so hard that she was finding it hard to breathe. He ran to get his mother because she always knew what to do. Mothers do. Children never stop to think why, they just know mothers can handle any situation and restore calm immediately. It must be biological because fathers, no matter how good they are, never seem to possess this magical power. Kathy took Chloe through to her room so that Jay could go back to sleep. He could still hear coughing as he drifted back into a dreamless slumber that seemed all too short.

He awoke around 7.30 and crept out to look in the other bedroom. Both Chloe and his mother were asleep, but judging by the state of the covers, they'd had a restless night. He decided the best thing he could do was to organise breakfast in bed for them. He tiptoed down the stairs, as quietly as a boy could, and walked through the lounge to the back of the house.

What was it that mum always did first? Switch on the kettle and make a pot of tea. He started to feel quite grown up as he collected cups and saucers, a tray and bowls for the cereal. Milk came next and as he poured himself a glassful, he spilt some down his pyjamas. He wiped it off with a tea towel and looked around for her apron. Back of the door, he thought – and there it was. Now he really looked the part. Just like one of the celebrity chefs on TV that his mum was always watching. He tied the straps around himself and tucked the ends into the pocket at the front. As he did, his hand touched something so he lifted it out. It was the number the girl had given him on the train. He looked at it for a moment and all at once decided he was going to make the call. Chloe had had a bad night, his mother was exhausted and this was the only thing he could think of to help, apart from making breakfast.

'Hello?' said the voice at the other end of the phone. It was a woman's voice, a friendly voice thought Jay, but still he didn't say anything. He didn't know what to say. 'Can I help you?' said the voice.

'My name is Jay, Jay Ashley from Barnoldswick ... or Barlick as we call it.' He wasn't quite sure why he had said all that, but he had, so it was too late.

'Yes?' said the voice.

Now what? thought Jay. What could he say that wouldn't make him sound totally crazy?

'I was given your number by a girl on the train who got off in Skipton and she told me I should call.' The words seemed to run together and he hoped that they made sense.

'Yes?' said the voice again.

'It's my sister,' he said. 'She is real sick and the

girl said you might be able to help.' He waited for an answer. He wasn't sure what answer, almost anything would do.

'My name is Maggie,' said the voice. 'Maggie Pendle. I live in Kelbrook, at High Trough Farm with my husband Seth. We take in sick children once in a while to give their parents a rest. Tell me more about your sister'.

Jay started to talk. It was like he was talking to the girl again. He seemed to be telling Maggie his life story. Not just his life story but that of his mother and sister as well, not forgetting his father. After a while he came to a halt.

'Well,' said Maggie, 'that is quite a tale. It certainly sounds as if your mother deserves a rest. The problem is that we hadn't really planned on anyone staying with us at the moment. I'm not sure we could take you.' Jay's heart sank. 'Let me talk it over with Seth and then I'll call you back.'

Maggie took Jay's number and then hung up, promising she would get back to him just as soon as Seth got back in from checking on the sheep.

Jay sat back on the kitchen stool. He hoped Maggie would call back. He hoped his mother wouldn't mind that he had called. He hoped that Maggie would be able to help, even if it was only so his mother could get a good night's sleep. He went back to making breakfast, which was perfect timing, as he heard movement upstairs.

He didn't mention the phone call to his mother until after she had eaten, showered and put on her clothes. He had also waited until Chloe had gone downstairs so that she wouldn't hear.

'Oh, Jay!' exclaimed his mother. 'We don't know these people from Adam. How could you?' She didn't seem very happy.

'I only did it for Chloe,' he said quickly.

'I know you did,' said his mother, a tear rolling down her cheek. 'It was very sweet of you. If this Maggie lady calls back I'll explain the situation and thank her for her time,' she said, not wanting to upset Jay who had obviously meant well.

Jay went in to watch TV with Chloe and waited for Maggie to call back. It seemed like an age before he heard the familiar ringing sound.

'I'll get it,' shouted his mother and the ringing stopped. It seemed like she talked forever before the click of the phone in the lounge signalled his mother had finished on the kitchen extension. Kathy walked in to where the children were sitting on the sofa.

'Get dressed,' she said. 'We're going to visit a farm'.

Chapter 3

Kathy, Chloe and Jay all bundled into their car. It was only a few minutes up the road, but they felt as if they were entering the unknown, particularly Kathy who still couldn't understand why she had agreed to visit the lady. Jay watched the dry stone walls passing by and wondered what Maggie had said to convince his mother to visit.

As they travelled along Kelbrook Road, Kathy explained to Chloe about the phone call and the reason for the visit. Chloe just sat there, saying nothing. She looked at Jay. He smiled a reassuring smile and she felt better. Kathy turned left at the roundabout and then took a right down Vicarage Lane. From there, on to Cob Lane. Maggie had said to pass Moor Gate and Thick Bank and the farm would be on the left – and there it was.

She pulled into the yard. It was obviously a working farm from the aroma and the noises coming from every corner.

As Kathy parked the car, an older lady appeared from the house and walked towards them. She was round in face and body, had grey curly hair and was exactly what you would expect your grand-mother to look like if you had never met her before. She had a beaming grin and greeted Kathy with a hug as if she had known her all her life.

'Come in, come in,' she chirped and herded them all into the kitchen. It was exactly how it should have looked. An old pine table, a big wood-burning stove, pies cooling on the window ledge and a jug of lemonade on the table. The children felt more than welcome – they felt at home somehow.

'Sit yourselves down,' said Maggie as she started to pour them each a glass from the jug. 'That's Seth,' she said, pointing to a photo of herself and a ruggedly good-looking elderly gentleman. Jay peered at the photo and thought he seemed vaguely familiar, but could not place him.

'It was taken last year at Gisburn market. He'll be down from the fields soon, I expect.'

Kathy scrutinised the picture, noticing how happy they both looked. Not just happy, she thought ... contented. Maggie started to talk and the time seemed to fly by. She told them about how she had lived there most of her life, how her daughter had grown up and moved away and how she now offered to look after sick children to help their parents have a few days' rest.

'Seems perfect to me,' said Maggie. 'You only live just down the road, so why don't you leave the children here, bring some clothes by later and have yourself a relaxing long weekend?'

To the delight and astonishment of the children, Kathy immediately agreed, thanked Maggie profusely and stood up.

'Be good for Maggie,' said Kathy as she hugged them both and then she turned to Maggie and gave her a hug too. A mixture of a 'thank you for under-standing' and an 'it's nice to be able to talk about it' hug.

She turned and walked out into the yard. A collie dog had appeared from the barn and it came jogging over to meet the children.

'That's Ben,' explained Maggie as Kathy started up the motor. 'He thinks he runs things around here.'

'I'll be back later with some clothes,' Kathy shouted, and in an instant she was gone.

Maggie turned and headed back into the farmhouse. 'Come on,' she shouted. 'Let's explore!'

The rest of the day sped by. Maggie showed them their room and all the other rooms in the rambling old house. It was fantastic! Old beams, secret doorways, three staircases and more places for hide-and-seek than you could ever dream of. Then there was the farmyard. A barn, four outbuildings, a collection of pens and holding areas for the sheep and wherever they walked – or ran in Jay's case – Ben padded alongside them. In truth he seemed to keep close to Chloe as if he knew she needed extra attention.

It was now late afternoon and Chloe was feeling very tired from the day's excitement.

'Time to take it easy now,' said Maggie as she led them back into the sitting room. 'You sit yourselves down and I'll make us some tea.'

Chloe turned to look at her brother. 'Thanks,' she said, hugging him tightly. She had not done that in years, not since they were really little. Jay smiled. Neither said another word. They didn't need to.

Maggie brought through some fresh bread and cheese, some home-grown tomatoes from the greenhouse and some onions she had pickled earlier that year. They ate heartily and washed it down with glasses of milk from the neighbouring farm. When they had finished, Jay helped to clear away the plates while Chloe rested.

It was then that Kathy reappeared with their suitcases. Jay hugged her as she entered the kitchen and Maggie smiled, taking the bags from her and placing them in the corner.

'I'll pick you up on Monday,' said Kathy, looking straight at Jay as if to say 'Behave and enjoy the fact that I am letting you do this'.

'Thanks, mum.'

'Be sure to get to bed early and have lots of rest this weekend.'

'Don't worry about Chloe,' said Jay, 'I'll look after her.'

There was no doubt in Kathy's mind. Jay was a good boy and he loved his sister, no matter what the bravado said. Kathy went into the lounge to say goodbye to Chloe and then she got in the car and drove off into the distance. Ben followed the car across the yard and down the road as if giving Kathy a royal send off.

The children decided to head off to bed and read a little before lights out. Maggie told them they could help themselves to any books they found on the bookshelves. There were so many. Chloe and Jay ran their fingers along the spines shelf-by-shelf, trying to guess what they were all about from their titles. Eventually Chloe found a book about training horses, something she had always dreamed of doing. Jay was drawn to a book entitled *Myths of the Pendle Hills*. They both washed and changed for bed. They each had a light on their bedside table so Maggie came in and turned off the main one.

'Just turn your lights off when you're ready,' she said, 'and I'll see you in the morning. We can all go to Gisburn market tomorrow, if you like. There will be lots of animals, so I'm sure you will have a good time.'

Chloe was the first to put her book down. 'I've had a great day,' she said as she turned off her light. 'I'm glad you made the call. Thanks.' She rolled over and said goodnight to Jay.

He was now entranced by stories of The Hill Folk. It seemed they were a little like druids and used to roam the moorland, living in stone shelters. They worshipped nature and believed in witches and wizards and all sorts of supernatural things. Eventually fatigue got the better of him and he turned off his light. He snuggled down between the sheets and quickly fell into a deep sleep.

Chapter 4

Maggie woke the children around nine o'clock. They had slept well, probably as well as they had slept in the last month. Chloe felt she had renewed energy and quickly washed and dressed, heading down to help Maggie with their breakfast. Maggie had been up for hours and said that Seth was already out across the fields.

After the children had eaten, Maggie made some sandwiches and put them, along with some bottled lemonade, into a basket. The three of them then climbed into Maggie's Land Rover and they set off down the hill towards Kelbrook.

Through Salterforth they travelled and then through Barnoldswick. Straight across at the mini roundabout by the school and then out through Bracewell. The children had lived in Foulridge for some time now, but rarely travelled out along these roads, so it was all new and exciting. Maggie turned left on to the A59 signposted to Gisburn and Clitheroe. After about five minutes she started to slow down, as the traffic was quite heavy.

'Farmers bringing their animals here to market,' Maggie explained, and the children looked at the trailers in front where the sheep were sticking their heads though the bars to see what was happening. They pulled into the market and parked with all the other farm vehicles. There was so much noise and so many smells. It was like a full frontal assault on the senses. Jay didn't know where to look first.

'Stay close,' said Maggie. 'I don't want to see you being auctioned off as livestock!'

She chuckled as she made her way across the car park and towards the holding pens. Chloe and Jay were both loving it. They were stroking sheep and cows, looking at cages of chickens, watching pens full of pigs head-butting each other and then Chloe looked into a horsebox and immediately fell in love. Inside was the most incredible sight she had ever seen: a tall chestnut mare with the most beautiful of eyes. It seemed to be looking straight back at Chloe and she felt as though she could look into those eyes and see her own soul.

'A beauty, ain't she?' said a voice behind her.

Chloe turned to see a man standing there, resting

on a shepherd's crook. He had a ruddy face, cloth cap and Wellingtons. Every inch the way Chloe thought a farmer should look.

'She's called Midnight Rose.'

Jay had now joined them. 'After The Midnight Rose in the legend?' he asked.

'That's right,' said the farmer. 'What do you know of the legend?'

'I read about it last night in a book at Maggie Pendle's,' he said, feeling quite grown up to be having such a conversation with this man. 'The Midnight Rose was supposed to be a magical rose that was the most beautiful thing that people had ever seen.'

'Then the name fits,' said Chloe as she ran her hand down the horse's cheek.

'It was also said to have amazing healing powers for those lucky enough to find it on Kelbrook Moor. The legend says that it only blooms at midnight and that you will never find it – it will find you,' added Jay, just to let the farmer know he knew his stuff.

'Very good,' said the farmer, 'except for one thing. You used the past tense. There are those around here that still believe it to be true. Many have searched the hills in vain looking for The Midnight Rose and I'm sure there will be plenty more yet.'

At that moment Maggie appeared and told the

children she had saved them seats in the auction room. They said goodbye to the farmer, Chloe gave the horse a final stroke and then they made their way to their seats.

It was the first time the children had seen an auction and they spent the first 15 minutes trying to see when someone made a bid. The auctioneer spoke so quickly and the bids were so difficult to see that 20 animals had come and gone before they started to notice who was bidding and how. Some tipped their caps, some nodded and some touched their noses. It was a great game, but Maggie warned them not to move around so much or they may find they had bought themselves a cow. Soon Chloe and Jay were in a competition to see who could guess the price the closest. Chloe won. Jay had no idea but didn't seem to mind. It was great to see his sister enjoying herself and forgetting all about her illness.

It was lunchtime before they knew it and Maggie suggested they leave the market and find a place to picnic. She drove them down Mill Lane to Gisburn Bridge and parked the car. She laid a blanket out on the bank of the river Ribble and the three of them tucked into the sandwiches while watching the water bubbling past in the sunshine. Chloe seemed relaxed, at peace.

'Maggie,' said Jay, 'what do you know about

The Midnight Rose?'

Maggie smiled. 'Oh,' she said, 'is that what you were talking to Dick Chapman about? Don't you pay any attention to him. Just tales and superstition.'

'Wouldn't it be wonderful if such a rose did grow on the moor?' murmured Chloe as she lay on her back looking at the pictures in the clouds.

'It certainly would,' said Maggie, 'but don't you go filling your head with wild dreams and flights of fancy, young lady,' she said with a mock scolding tone.

Chloe laughed and started to tear the crusts off her sandwiches to feed to the growing number of ducks that were making their way up the bank.

Jay had rolled his trouser legs up and was wading in the shallow water along the river's edge.

He had left the 'women folk' and had gone exploring on his own. 'Man's work,' he told himself. He was lifting stones and seeing what swam out, the perfect pastime for most 11 year olds. You can forget about trying to be older than you are and just enjoy the moment.

He saw a stickleback out of the corner of his eye and made a lunge to catch it. His foot slipped and he began to tumble forward. He grabbed at a large rock that was sticking out of the bank, but it started to shift under his weight. The next thing he knew was that he was under water. He couldn't get up. He had a pain in his chest and felt an incredible pressure pushing on his ribs. He opened his eyes. He could see the surface of the water. He could reach up with his hand and break through to the air but he couldn't move, couldn't breathe.

Then he realised the awful truth. The rock had fallen into the river after him and had landed on his chest, pinning him helplessly on the bed of the river. There was nothing he could do. He couldn't shout for help. He couldn't move the rock. He couldn't even think!

Then he saw a hand. He grabbed it and managed to pull himself up enough so that the rock slipped off his chest and into the mud at the bottom of the river. His head broke the surface and his lungs sucked in the beautiful air that his body craved. He coughed up some river water and threw himself on to the bank, panting for all he was worth.

'It's dangerous to play in the river alone,' said a voice.

He raised his head enough to see a pair of shoes standing next to him. Not big shoes he noticed. He looked up, partly blinded by the sun, and studied the face of his saviour. It was a young girl.

'Are you OK?' she asked in a concerned voice.

'Thanks,' said Jay, still gasping for breath. 'Thanks for pulling me out. You saved my life.'

The girl smiled. 'Just be more careful, will you?' and then without another word she turned and ran up the bank and out of his sight.

The next moment Maggie and Chloe appeared by his side.

'What happened to you?' asked Chloe. 'You're soaking wet. Did you fall in?'

Jay decided not to worry them. 'Yes, pretty stupid really.'

'Time to get you home,' said Maggie and she marched him back to the picnic site, threw the blanket around him and steered him back to the Land Rover with her arm around him to keep him warm.

Later, back at the farmhouse after he had showered and changed, Jay told Chloe what had really happened. She looked horrified.

'You might have drowned,' she cried.

Jay took no notice of her concern. 'I know this is going to sound really strange,' he said, 'but I'm sure the girl who saved me was the same girl that was on the train.'

Chapter 5

The children awoke to the smell of bacon. It's the sort of smell that when you get older brings back wonderful memories of childhood. The sort of smell that turns a house into a home. The sort of smell that finds every nook and cranny, leaving no place untouched. Chloe and Jay leapt out of bed and ran downstairs to the kitchen.

'I thought this might get you up,' laughed Maggie who had freshly baked bread, scrambled eggs and grilled field mushrooms to add to the feast. 'I always cook well for Seth on a Sunday morning. Gives him the energy to go and tend the sheep on the high moor,' she said, sliding the rashers out on to three plates.

They all tucked into a meal fit for a king. Ben kept guard under the table in case anything was dropped and needed cleaning up, but to his increasing dismay everyone seemed to be eating very tidily that morning.

Eventually Chloe passed him some bacon rind and Ben relaxed, lying across her feet to let her know he was there if needed to help out with any more scraps.

'Maggie,' Jay said with a slightly quizzical tone to his voice, 'I was reading some more about the legend of The Midnight Rose last night'.

Maggie smiled. 'And you have a question?' she retorted as if reading his mind. Jay thought for a while.

'Is there any truth to it?'

'Well,' she started, 'there are folk who will tell you that all legends are based on the truth and those who will tell you it is nothing but gossip made up over the centuries and embellished over pints of beer at the tavern.'

Chloe smiled. Maggie seemed so old-fashioned sometimes. She had only ever heard people refer to it as a 'tavern' in old movies on TV.

'But what do *you* think, Maggie?' asked Jay, determined to get a better answer than the one she had given.

'There are certainly many tales around these parts,' she said, 'and it does make you wonder if they can all be made up. My grandma used to tell me tales of The Hill Folk when I were young. How the women used to cure the villagers with ancient medicines handed down from generation to generation and how the men would help the farmers when the animals got sick. There are tales of witches and wizards, goblins and fairy folk and stories that defy the imagination. I suppose a part of me wants to believe they are true and it all certainly helps the local tourist trade!' She laughed and slid another slice of bacon on to Jay's plate.

'Have you or Seth ever seen anything unusual up on the moor?' he asked, not wanting to let the subject drop.

'I suppose it depends on what you mean by unusual,' Maggie said as she took her plate over to the sink. 'I have seen dancing lights at dusk and heard voices when I have been walking with Ben, but never seen a soul to go with them.'

Jay looked at her, wanting to hear more.

'Seth has seen some strange goings on, particularly in lambing season, but you'd better ask him yourself.'

Jay looked a little disappointed. 'Now that I think about it,' said Maggie, obviously struggling to bring back a fairly ancient memory, 'it does bring to mind an incident that happened here at the Lower Meadow when I was about your age. I was walking with Jess – he was my father's sheep dog –

when I heard a rustling in the grass nearby. Jess laid down and was just staring at a clump of marsh reeds. I could hardly breathe and then my heart nearly stopped when I saw a small pair of eyes looking back at me.'

Jay shifted in his seat. 'What did they look like?'

'Kind of like a frog's, yellow with a deep black pupil. Suddenly they darted to one side and Jess pounced. I ran over to see what he had caught, but the creature had moved too quickly. Jess ran around trying to herd it, like a sheep, but each time it seemed to get away.'

Chloe was transfixed, her fork stationary midway between her plate and her mouth.

'I decided the only way was to try and catch it in my small fishing net that I used to catch tadpoles in, so I ran back to the farm to get it. When I got back, Jess had driven it in to the corner of the field and had it pinned in the long grass up against the dry stone wall. All I could see were the bright eyes boring out from the foliage.' She paused for effect.

'I raised the net above my head and then brought it crashing down, holding it with all my might as the creature lurched this way and that, trying to escape its unexpected confinement.'

Jay's eyes had widened. Now they were getting somewhere. Now he was going to find out what sort of animals were roaming on the moors.

'Afraid that it might bite me, but more afraid that it might escape,' continued Maggie, 'I thrust my hand under the net.'

As she said it, she thrust her hand across the table, causing Chloe to scream, drop her fork and fall sideways off her chair. Ben leapt up as Chloe came crashing down next to him, but then he noticed the fork and the food and Chloe was soon forgotten.

Maggie helped Chloe back to the table.

'What was it?' asked Jay, almost in a whisper. 'What did you find?'

'Well,' said Maggie thoughtfully, 'I peeked through my fingers and those yellow eyes were staring back menacingly. I decided to lift my top hand away quickly so that I could get a good look at it before it realised it could escape, because then it would be gone forever.'

Jay could feel his heart pounding in his chest.

'And,' asked both children in unison, 'what was it?'

'A frog!' exclaimed Maggie triumphantly, as Chloe burst in to peals of laughter, closely followed by Jay.

Chloe and Jay finished eating and Maggie then sent them upstairs to get dressed. When they reached their room Chloe turned to Jay.

'I know this sounds strange, but I'm going to go

back to bed. I really feel quite tired.'

Jay looked at his sister and smiled. 'Don't worry about it, Chloe,' he said, trying to sound comforting yet unconcerned. 'You've been going at it pretty hard since we got here.'

Chloe slid back under the sheets and Jay pulled the thick floral curtains. The room was once again shrouded in darkness. He quickly put on his clothes, kissed his sister on the forehead and said he would check on her later. He bounded down the stairs and went straight into the kitchen to see Maggie.

'I'm worried,' he said as Maggie passed him a freshly brewed cup of tea. 'It seems as though she's getting weaker day by day.'

Maggie smiled a reassuring smile. 'Well, *don't* worry,' she said soothingly. 'She'll have good days and bad days. She will tire easily and you two have been going nineteen to the dozen since you got here.'

Jay felt a little better, but he was still worried deep down inside. He knew Maggie was right but all he wanted was for Chloe to get better.

Kathy had spent most of Saturday doing house-work. She dusted, vacuumed, folded laundry and changed the sheets on the three beds. All the time she was asking herself why she had let them go to Maggie's. After all, she was a complete stranger.

Someone she had met through a phone number from a girl on a train. This was so unlike her. Since Peter had died she had been incredibly protective of the children – overly protective, if the truth were known. When she had first spoken to Maggie it had been with the intention of politely refusing her offer, but within hours they had all been at the farm unloading suitcases. Maggie appeared so kind, so understanding that it just seemed right.

By early evening she had made herself some pasta and a salad. So nice not to have something fried, she thought to herself as, like most single parents, she tended to eat an extension of whatever the children ate. She celebrated the peace and quiet with a glass of white wine – a rare treat – and snuggled down on the sofa wondering what Chloe and Jay were up to.

She had then awoken and looked at the clock. 11:30pm! She had fallen asleep watching the Saturday movie. Slowly she raised herself up and switched off the TV. She put her dishes in the sink, vowing to wash them first thing in the morning, and crept up the stairs to bed. Why am I creeping up the stairs? she asked herself. This had been the first time that the kids had stayed away from home since Peter's accident. Kathy brushed her teeth, slipped into her nightdress and with a contented sigh climbed into bed.

'Nothing like your own bed,' she said as she closed her eyes and immediately fell into a deep sleep.

Chapter 6

Kathy came to with a start as if coming out of that dream where you are falling and just about to hit the ground. You never do though. The phone was ringing. She glanced at the clock by the bed. 10:50am. She had never slept that long in her life. Well, not since she was a teenager. Obviously Maggie had been right. Her body needed the rest. Kathy leant over and answered the phone by her bed.

'Mrs Ashley?' enquired the voice. 'Mrs Kathy Ashley?' Kathy didn't recognise the man on the other end.

'Who is this, please?' she asked, never wanting to give away the advantage to a stranger.

'Dr Silcock from St James' Hospital in Leeds.' Kathy's heart nearly stopped.

'We promised we would call as soon as we had some information to give you,' he continued. Kathy couldn't speak. 'Are you there?' he asked. 'Are you there, Mrs Ashley?'

Kathy was afraid to answer. Afraid of what he might tell her. For years she had wanted an explanation of why Chloe was always so tired, but now she was so close to getting the answer it scared her. All she could think was 'What if ...?'

'Yes, I'm here,' she croaked back into the mouthpiece.

'We have had the test results back on Chloe,' explained the doctor. 'If you would prefer you can come in and I'll take you through them face-to-face.'

Kathy's mind began to race. Why would they want her to come in if it wasn't bad news? she thought, her mind reeling with the sentence and its ramifications.

'Can't you just tell me over the phone?' she asked, sitting on the side of her bed, feeling more alone than she had in years.

'Of course I can,' he said, 'it's just that some people prefer to talk about such things in person.'

His voice was calm and it put Kathy a little more at ease.

'I understand that your local doctor has been

treating Chloe with vitamins and iron tablets for a couple of years now and that only recently did you seek a second opinion, is that right?' he asked.

'That's right,' said Kathy, hating herself for not questioning their doctor sooner. People never questioned doctors. It simply wasn't done when she was growing up. Doctors were close to God in the mind of her parents. Rarely were they wrong, if ever, and certainly never to be doubted.

'I'm afraid that ...'

Kathy never heard the rest of the sentence. No sentence that started that way ever had a happy ending. She started to sob uncontrollably.

'Are you all right?' asked the voice at the other end of the phone.

What a wasted question. Of course she was not all right.

Chapter 7

Jay had decided to go exploring on his own while Chloe slept. He left the farmyard and headed out through the field of sheep. The sun was starting to burn through one of those early morning mists that made the valley look like a lake. He turned and looked down the hill towards the Old Stone Trough pub. He could see nothing beyond the roof of the farmhouse. The mist swirled in the same way that water moves as it picks its way down a mountain stream.

Jay felt as though he could have launched a boat from where he stood and sailed across to Salterforth. 'Magical' is the only way to describe this sight and if you have never had the privilege of seeing such a mist, you must travel to the hills before too much longer so that you can understand.

Jay turned and continued his way across the pasture. The grass was wet, so wet that his shoes and socks were quickly soaked through. He didn't care. The air was so clear that everything seemed in sharper focus than he had ever seen it before. The sky was blue, a deep azure blue, and the few clouds that were dotted around the sky were drifting effortlessly towards the horizon.

He could hear skylarks singing their distinctive song and the gentle, almost motor-like buzz of innumerable insects that were busily rushing from here to there. The sheep were acting as though this was just another day. But then again, what did sheep know? thought Jay to himself.

Climbing up on top of the stile that straddled the gritstone wall, Jay surveyed all that he could see. He felt like the captain of a four-masted schooner looking out over the ocean, trying to decide in which direction the next adventure lay. He stopped a while to watch a peacock butterfly that was moving from rock to rock as if looking for exactly the right place to rest. The colours were so vibrant in the sun and Jay felt at peace with the world for the first time since learning about Chloe's problem.

Looking up the hill, Jay plotted his next course. Across the marshy tranche of fell that lay between him and the heather and then on upward to the peak of the hill.

Before falling asleep last night, Jay had spent over an hour with his book on local folklore and was determined to find out more about The Midnight Rose. He wanted to believe the story so much because he just knew that its magical healing powers could help his sister. In his heart of hearts he knew that it was likely to be just a story, but what if it wasn't?

He had read about how The Hill Folk used to meet in stone circles when they were holding council. The stones were placed in areas where the force of the earth was felt to be the strongest so that it would help them to channel energy into any medicine that was being prepared, or any decision that needed to be taken. They were firm believers in the power of nature and spent more time harnessing what it had to offer than worrying about how it worked.

Doctors could learn a lot from them, thought Jay to himself.

He set off across the marsh, jumping from tuft of grass to tuft of grass. He remembered being told that it was likely to be less damp and soggy where the marsh grass grew in clumps. He couldn't remember who had told him, but they obviously knew their stuff. He was across in no time and with feet no wetter than when he started. He was now at the edge of the moorland proper. Ahead of him lay a great open expanse of heather and scrub although he could see no way across it. He knew there had to be a path somewhere, but where exactly?

It looked impossible to cut across so Jay started to walk along its edge hoping to find a way through. Even a sheep track would do, he thought to himself as he plucked a piece of the purple heather and narrowly avoided getting stung by a rather disgruntled bee!

Eventually he found a break in the scrub, or at least he convinced himself he had found one. He started to push his way through the coarse under-growth hoping that it would widen into a better path. It didn't. The rough squat bushes were scratching at his ankles as he slowly forced his way through. He wished he had put on his jeans rather than his shorts, but it was too late now. He was a man on a mission and nothing was going to stop him, at least not for the moment. He felt fairly sure that unless things improved he might change his mind, but for the moment he was adamant.

After some twenty painful minutes, when he noticed that his legs were now in fact bleeding, he decided to take a rest. Before him was a slightly less aggressive looking patch of foliage, so he sat down as best he could. He decided that he deserved a rest after his exertions so he laid back, hands clasped behind his head, and looked up into the sky.

The first cloud he saw looked exactly like a dragon's head. It must be something to do with boys, because no matter what shape a cloud might be, they can always make out a dragon. Next came Winnie the Pooh, closely followed by a pirate ship. Imagination is a wonderful thing isn't it? He was just deciding whether the big feathery looking one reminded him more of a chicken or his fifth grade teacher when a voice said:

'That one looks like a parrot to me.'

Jay sat up, wondering who had spoken those words. He saw a shadow move in front of him so he quickly turned around to see who was making it. He saw a figure, but was having difficulty making out any detail, as he was now looking straight in to the sun. He lifted his right hand to shield the glare and rested on his left.

'I'm sorry,' said the voice. 'How rude of me to interrupt you and then to stand in the sun.'

The figure moved around to stand in front of Jay and introduced herself.

'I'm Margaret,' she said, holding out a hand to Jay.

He wasn't quite sure if he was supposed to shake it or use it to pull himself up, so he decided to shake it politely.

'Jay,' he said. 'Jay Ashley'.

'I'm very pleased to meet you, Jay,' said Margaret who, as Jay had just noticed, had the most amazing smile. Indeed, now he did not have the sun streaming into his eyes, he could see she was a stunning woman, probably in her twenties.

'Mind if I join you?' She sat herself down on the ground next to him. 'I love days like this,' she said, lying down in the heather looking up at the clouds. 'The world seems so simple up here. No noise, no worries, no people. The most important decision to make is whether that cloud looks like a chicken or a teacher from school.'

How did she know what I was thinking? thought Jay, suddenly feeling a little spooked.

'I come here most days when the sun is shining,' continued Margaret. 'It feels great to get close to nature, don't you think?'

Jay just looked at her. 'How did you know what I was thinking?' he asked, hoping that this was not too forward a question.

Margaret laughed. 'Are your ankles sore? I know mine are. It helps if you rub this on.'

She picked a broad-leafed plant that Jay hadn't seen before and started rubbing it on to his scratches. She was right. The cuts and scrapes immediately stopped itching and the pain started to subside.

'What brings you on to the moor?' she asked,

still looking skyward, her eyes half closed.

'Nothing really,' replied Jay, not wanting to seem too weird being out here looking for a mythical plant. Margaret laughed again.

'Please,' she said, 'no one forces their way through the heather for no reason. Either you are very lost or are very serious about finding something. You certainly don't look lost, so you must be on a quest.'

Jay wondered why she had chosen the word 'quest'. It made it sound like something from a Harry Potter novel. How should he answer? He sat there for a moment and then turned to Margaret.

'If I tell you a secret, will you promise not to laugh?'

Margaret looked back at him, her face lit by the morning sun.

'I promise,' she said and Jay started to explain about his sister, the book, the market and as a crowning detail, The Midnight Rose.

Jay must have talked nonstop for fifteen minutes and in that entire time Margaret had said nothing. Eventually Jay ground to a halt, almost embarrassed about telling a complete stranger his life story.

'Wow,' said Margaret, 'that *is* quite a story.' She did not judge, she did not comment, she just lay there for a minute.

'What makes you think your Midnight Rose is up here?'

Jay explained how he had been reading a book at Maggie's house and that it had talked about The Hill Folk and the medicinal plants that could be found up on the moor. He had tied in the story he had heard from the farmer at Gisburn market with the places mentioned in the book and had decided that this was the place to find the plant.

'Do you think you can only find the plant at midnight?' asked Margaret. 'Or do you think that it is just the name?'

Jay looked at her for a moment. The awful truth was that he had never even given it a thought. He was so determined to find the magical flower to help his sister and he was so sure that it must be on the moor where they were sitting, that he had never considered the time element. Margaret seemed to know that he was struggling with some inner dilemma and decided to break the silence.

'If it helps, I can tell you that I have heard tales of The Hill Folk and how they used to come up on to the moor of an evening. They would meet up on certain days of the year, predetermined by the cycles of the moon, or if they had a particular problem to solve. The stories speak of a stone circle, one for each member of the group and a centre stone that was the seat of the most powerful member of The Hill Folk. If there was a particularly sick person from the local community they would be brought into the circle and The Hill Folk would work their magic of herbs and incantations to cure the illness. Then they would be returned to their families. However, they were told never to reveal the whereabouts of the circle, what had happened to them or who was there, for if they did, the illness would return and there would be no further cure.'

Jay listened intently. This was more information than he had found in his books and wanted Margaret to tell him more.

'There's not much more to tell,' she said, plucking a piece of heather and sliding it behind her ear. 'I have also heard of The Midnight Rose, but sadly I cannot give you any more information than you already have. I *can* tell you, though, that in all the years I have come up on to the moor I have never seen anything that looks like it would be called a Midnight Rose. I know a lot of plants from around these parts, but I have never seen a picture of what you are looking for.'

Jay smiled. 'Not to worry,' he said, 'I know it's here somewhere and I'm sure I will find it.'

Margaret looked at him thoughtfully. 'Something tells me you will.'

In an instant she was on her feet. 'It was really nice meeting you,' she said, holding out her hand again, 'but I'm afraid I must be away. I have a husband to feed and a thousand things to do today. I hope you find what you are looking for.'

She turned and started to walk away. Jay watched the ease with which she walked through the coarse heather and how the sun seemed to reflect off every part of her body, almost giving her an angelic glow. Suddenly she turned and looked back at Jay.

'Just remember,' she said. 'often things are closer than you think.'

Jay wanted to ask what she meant, but as he jumped to his feet he tripped on something hard and he fell to his knees. When he had regained his balance and looked up, she had gone.

Chapter 8

Back at the farm, Chloe was still resting in her room. Little did she know that downstairs her mother was pouring her heart out to Maggie.

'It's all so unfair,' she sobbed, her face red and streaked with mascara. 'If only our doctor had admitted he didn't know what was wrong with her and had sent Chloe for tests at the beginning.'

Maggie put her arm around Kathy to comfort her and Kathy buried her head into Maggie's shoulder, the same way she had done with her own mother when she was Chloe's age. The warmth of human contact was reassuring and Kathy had missed it since Peter's death.

'Be strong, Kathy,' said Maggie as she gently stroked her hair. 'Never give up hope. New miracle cures are being found all the time and you never know what might be around the corner.'

Kathy attempted to smile. She knew Maggie was trying to help, but the doctor had been very direct. He had left her in no doubt that things looked bleak, very bleak indeed. She had insisted that the doctor gave it to her straight and that is exactly what he had done. Kathy had been ready for bad news, or so she had thought, but nothing could have prepared her for the news that she had received.

'He told me that we had only a matter of weeks, perhaps a few months at the most.'

Floods of tears were again running down her face. She was unable to carry on speaking, as the words seemed to catch in her throat. Eventually she regained control.

'How am I ever going to tell Jay?' Maggie handed her a fresh cup of tea. 'How am I ever going to tell Chloe? Children are not supposed to die before their parents, it's just not fair!'

Maggie held Kathy's hand and they sat on the sofa together for the longest time without saying a thing. There was nothing to be said. Who could argue with Kathy's last words?

Maggie looked up at the ceiling. She could hear stirrings from the children's room. Chloe was up now and moving around.

'I don't want her to see me like this,' said Kathy,

quickly getting to her feet. 'I need some time to let this all sink in and decide how to tell them. Can I leave them here with you for a little while longer? I'm going back to Leeds tomorrow to see the specialist again. I hope that he can tell me something more.'

Secretly she was hoping that he was going to say it had all been a terrible mistake and that the diagnosis had been completely wrong. She wanted to hear that Chloe was going to be all right. She wanted to hear how she would live a long and happy life, how she would marry and have kids and enjoy everything that life had to offer. She also knew that this was not going to happen.

Kathy hugged Maggie as if she had been a lifelong friend and kissed her gently on the cheek.

'Leave them here as long as you want,' she said. 'Seth and me will look after them.'

Kathy made her way across the farmyard with Ben at her heels, as always. She got into her car and with a wave to Maggie standing in the kitchen doorway she pulled out into the lane and headed back to Barlick.

As Jay made his way down off the moor he kept thinking about the words that Margaret had uttered just before she disappeared.

'Often things are closer than you think.' What

had she meant by that? Did she know something about what he was searching for? Was she just being nice?

Was she trying to tell him something? Jay's mind was racing all the way back across the fields to the farm.

Should he tell Maggie of his chance meeting or not? Should he tell Chloe? In the end he decided that he would tell no one. He wanted to find what he was looking for before he raised any hopes. There was no doubt in his mind that The Midnight Rose existed and that if he could only find it, it would help his sister. His conviction was one hundred percent – he had never been so sure of anything before in his life.

Ben ran across the last field to greet him and knocked him down in his eagerness to welcome him back. Whether you had been gone ten minutes or a full day, it was all the same to Ben – he was just pleased to have you back.

Jay rolled around on the floor with him and Ben barked and jumped with excitement. The sheep grazing nearby seemed completely unperturbed by all the carrying on, having grown used to it over the years.

Maggie looked out the window, knowing that it must be Jay coming back, and immediately poured out a cool glass of lemonade.

'You must be hungry,' she said as Jay stopped to take off his shoes before padding his way into the warmth of the kitchen. 'Did you have a good walk?' She started to slice some bread off the end of a freshly baked loaf.

There is something about the smell of fresh bread that defies description. It has an almost therapeutic effect on most people. It bestows a feeling of wellbeing. It reminds people of their childhoods, even if their mothers never baked bread!

Jay soaked in the aroma and sat down at the table. He drank deeply and wiped off the dampness that clung to his upper lip. Ben was now sitting at his side, ready to help out in case whatever was about to be eaten was going to be shared around. Jay cut a hunk of cheese off the block of farmhouse cheddar on the plate in the centre of the table and crumbled a small piece for Ben. The door to the lounge opened and in walked Chloe.

'I cannot believe I slept most of the day,' she said almost apologetically.

'You obviously needed it,' replied Maggie. 'Did you good to get some rest.'

The three of them sat around the table and talked as families did before television. The children asked Maggie about her life as a child and wanted to know all about what her school had been like when she was their age.

The time flew by and Jay and Chloe sat spell-bound as Maggie regaled them with tales of her youth. How she spent every waking hour up on the moor and how she never missed a market day. She seemed to have a faraway look in her eye as she spoke and it was obvious that she missed those days.

Jay studied her animated face and somehow felt sure that it was not her youth that she was missing, but the gentler, less complicated life when people had time to appreciate what the world had to offer and when people took the time to enjoy it. His mum had often bemoaned the fact that every-thing was too easy these days and that nobody truly appreciated what they had. She was always telling them to slow down and smell the roses and now, probably for the first time, Jay understood what she meant.

He looked across at Chloe, who seemed to be totally transfixed by Maggie's stories. She looked almost as if she had a halo, as her blonde hair was being backlit by the fading sun. There was colour in her cheeks, which had been unusual recently and made Jay feel good about life. It also made him promise himself that he would redouble his efforts in the morning. He was determined that he would find the flower and make Chloe well again. He was determined to rectify the awful error that the doctor had made and to see his sister live to a ripe old age.

That evening he pored over the old books that Maggie had on her bookshelf to glean any new piece of information about The Hill Folk, The Midnight Rose or any other small detail that might help him in his 'quest', as Margaret had called it. While he was totally immersed in his reading, Chloe lay on the floor in front of the fire, curled up with Ben, listening to a story read by Maggie. Ben almost looked as if he knew what the tale was about and every now and then would shift his head just enough to plant a huge wet kiss on Chloe's cheek. Each time it happened she would giggle and Maggie would look up from the pages and smile.

The fire gently hissed in the background and the smoke swirled as it was caught in the updraft and sent spiralling up the chimney, out into the chill night air. There is little more comforting than the glow of a well-established fire in the grate and Chloe seemed to be more at peace than she had been for months. She lay now with her head resting on Ben's back and looked up at Maggie who was sitting in her favourite chair between the hearth and the window.

She had told them it was her favourite, as from there she could see Seth coming in from the fields and also tell what the weather was likely to do by what she could see on the hilltops. She had an amazingly accurate way of gauging what was about to happen by which trees and bushes she could see, what shape the clouds were taking and how far she could see across the valley. Sometimes she seemed to be able to tell from the stars as well, and Chloe was quite sure that there was some magic involved, as she had not been wrong since their arrival.

Maggie stood up. 'Hot chocolate anyone?'

What an unnecessary question! Both children shouted with delight and skipped into the kitchen behind her. Maggie's chocolate was something else magical. It was so rich because of the fresh milk she used and the fact that she topped it off with whipped cream and sprinkles of cocoa and cinnamon. The whole house seemed to breathe in the aroma as it wafted its way from the kitchen into the lounge and then up the stairs to the bedroom.

Maggie reached for the tin that sat atop the larder and opened it for the children to choose their favourite biscuits. All freshly baked; nothing store-bought here. Maggie was the most wonderful cook and each bite seemed to melt in the children's mouths. Ben was also a great admirer of Maggie's talents, but tonight he was going to be out of luck. Jay and Chloe ate their fill and returned to the lounge for the last few minutes of the story.

Having nourished their body and soul, they wished Maggie a good night and followed the lingering smell of chocolate up the stairs and into the bedroom.

Chapter 9

True to his promise, Jay awoke with only one thing on his mind. He was going to get back out on to the moor, retrace his steps to where he had met Margaret the day before and redouble his efforts to find The Midnight Rose.

He looked at the clock on his bedside cabinet. 6:45. He glanced over at Chloe who was still fast asleep. She seemed so peaceful lying there, as there was no doubt to Jay that the dream world was where she could escape from the concerns that the daybreak would bring.

He dressed quietly and planted a gentle kiss on his sister's cheek. With his shoes in his hands, he crept out of the room and to the top of the stairs. He was hoping to leave a note on the table explaining that he had gone out early and that

Maggie should not worry as he would be back soon after lunch. When he reached the kitchen it became obvious he would have to change his plan.

'You're up early, young'n,' said Maggie, who was standing at the range already cooking breakfast. 'I thought you might like a little something in your stomach if you are going out exploring'.

Jay just looked at her. How had she known his plans? He was sure he had not said anything when he got back yesterday. He pulled a chair up to the table and Maggie dished out three rashers of bacon and two fried eggs. Jay started to eat them, not knowing if he should say something or just let the time pass until he could put on his shoes and head out across the fields.

'I reckon it must be something really important to get a young boy like you out of his bed at this time of the morning,' said Maggie as she cradled a cup of coffee in her two hands, gently sipping at the boiling hot contents. 'It's your business where you are heading off to, so don't feel you have to explain. All I would ask is that you take care, as there are all sorts of things up on the moor that can lead you into trouble. Be true to your heart and you'll be fine.'

Jay said nothing. He finished his breakfast, pulled on his shoes and walked over to Maggie.

'Thanks,' was all he could say and he hugged her

as hard as he had ever hugged anyone before.

Maggie held him closely and planted a kiss on the top of his head before releasing him. He walked over to the back door, stopping only to pat Ben who was standing there as if to wish him well. The sun had just made its way up over the hilltops and it was one of those magical mornings that most people will never see. The dew was glistening like a thousand diamonds, reflecting and refracting the light so that it sparkled with all the colours of the rainbow.

Jay's shoes were already soaking and he left a trail of footprints in the grass as he made his way across the meadow. The emerging shadows were incredibly long as the sun was so low in the sky. The air was clear and crisp and Jay could see his breath as he turned and headed up the hill to the side of the moor. There was not a cloud in the sky, but as he looked over the valley to Salterforth he could see the trail of a jet, cutting through the ether as if someone had taken a knife to a block of butter.

He made his way over the stile, stopping to drink in the beauty of his surroundings. He looked upward to the edge of the grassland where it met the heather. He tried to remember where he had made his way through yesterday so that he would not cut his ankles as badly as he had previously.

He had come prepared though, and had put on two pairs of his thickest and longest socks. He now bent down to tuck his trousers into their tops to try and keep the scrub from taking its toll. Looking around, Jay was delighted to see that the sun was shining down on the moorside and seemed to be illuminating the path that he had taken yesterday.

He ran across to make sure that the light was not playing tricks on him and then set off into the centre of the harsh brush. Within minutes he had come to the spot where he had met Margaret the day before. Jay sat himself down on a tuft of heather and started to cast around, looking for anything that might give him a clue. The problem was that everything appeared exactly the same in whichever direction he looked. The damp purple of the heather, the brown green colour of the cotton grass that poked its way up through the scrub and the white tufts that grew out of the top, like a rabbit's tail.

In the distance he could see a few trees that had been ravaged by centuries of vicious biting winds, leaning over at incredible angles as if they were trying to escape from the continual battering that they must receive on a daily basis. Jay strained his eyes to try and find something – anything – that would give him a clue as to where he should go next. Nothing. The frustration was building and

Jay began to think that the whole world was against him finding what he needed so desperately to find. In a growing rage he kicked out at the heather and in an instant he collapsed in the most searing pain. His foot had contacted with something solid. So solid, in fact, that he thought he had broken one – if not all – of the toes on his right foot. He lay on the floor with tears welling up in his eyes. He wanted to cry, but somehow kept his composure as he removed his shoe and rubbed his reddened, swelling toes.

'That has got to hurt,' came a voice from nowhere, stating the obvious. Jay turned and looked up through watery eyes to see who had appeared. He was sure that no one had been there moments before, when he had lost his temper and lashed out at the heather. How could he have missed someone? There was nowhere to hide, no trees, no boulders, no sinkholes that he could see.

'Let me have a look at that, Jay,' said the stranger. Jay was astonished to hear his name. Then he recognised the figure. It was Margaret.

'You're up early this morning,' she said as she gently knelt beside him, taking his swelling foot in her hands. 'Couldn't sleep?' She kneaded his toes, checking each one to see if it was broken.

'I've come back up to finish my quest,' said Jay, picking his words carefully to use the same term that Margaret had used the day before.

'Ah!' she said knowingly. 'Still looking for The Midnight Rose, eh?' Margaret reached out and grabbed what looked like a handful of moss, carefully pulling it from the ground so as to keep the moisture within the sponge-like body of the plant. She then plucked a few leaves off a very scrubby looking piece of vegetation nearby and folded the two together. Having rolled them into a ball in her hands, she placed them on Jay's toes and held them there while she continued to talk to him.

'How did this happen?' she asked, probably trying to take his mind off the throbbing pain in his foot, thought Jay.

'I came back up here because of what you said yesterday. As you left, you turned and said, 'often things are closer than you think', so I came back here to exactly the same spot to see if you were right.'

'And did you find anything?' asked Margaret almost matter of factly.

'Nothing,' said Jay, taking another swipe at the heather, but this time with his hand. 'Nothing at all.'

'Is that a fact?' Margaret was removing the compress that she had been holding on his toes. 'How does that feel now?'

Jay was amazed. The pain in his foot had all but

gone and the redness and swelling had disappeared almost as fast as it had arrived.

'That's incredible,' he said as he wiggled his toes around without feeling nauseous. 'How did you do that?'

Margaret seemed to ignore his question, choosing instead to return to her own that he had not answered previously.

'Why is it that you think you have found nothing?'

Jay didn't understand the question. It was quite obvious that there was nothing for miles around where they sat and he could not comprehend why she was asking this.

'Have you not discovered something unexpected?' continued Margaret.

'What do you mean?' Jay still didn't understand what she could be getting at.

'It seems to me that you were not expecting to break your toe when you kicked the heather just now,' said Margaret with a slight smile on her lips.

Jay laughed. 'That's true,' he said, sliding his damp socks back on over his now slightly pink toes.

'So ...' said Margaret as if trying to lead him to some conclusion.

'So what?' Jay was still struggling to see where this conversation was going.

'So what did you kick?' said Margaret in such a way that Jay felt quite stupid for not following her line of thought.

He had absolutely no idea what had been underneath the heather. He had been too busy wondering if he was ever going to walk again! Without saying anything he started to part the scrub with his hands in an attempt to uncover what had inflicted the injury on him.

Margaret looked over his shoulder as something slowly came into sight. Jay's heart was racing. Was this going to be what he had been looking for? Was this what Margaret had meant when she left him there on the moor yesterday?

As quickly as the excitement had built, it suddenly ebbed away. His shoulders dropped in disappointment as he finished uncovering a rock, a simple piece of limestone. He'd had such hopes that this was going to be something magical; the skull of a prehistoric beast perhaps, or an ancient flask containing an enchanted elixir that would cure his sister. All hopes dashed, he turned to Margaret.

'It's just a rock,' he said, his obvious disappointment showing on his face and in his voice.

Margaret looked back sympathetically.

'Ah well,' she said philosophically. 'Not everything we seek comes in the form we expect.'

What exactly did she mean this time? thought Jay to himself. Last time she had made a comment like that he had dismissed it at first, but then returned to the moor to follow it up. This time he was not going to be so stupid.

Jay started to examine the rock, because there was some reason Margaret had made that comment. It didn't seem very special. It was about two feet across in one direction, about a foot in the other and about a foot was showing above the ground. It was just a piece of limestone, no incredible fossils, no sign of any precious stones, just limestone with a couple of depressions on the top surface.

'What do you see?' asked Margaret in the same tone she had used before when trying to guide Jay through his search.

'Just a piece of limestone.'

'Anything special about it?'

'Not that I can see,' he said, knowing that he must be missing something.

Margaret offered Jay her hand. He took it and she pulled him to his feet. 'What do you see over there?' she asked. Jay looked across the moor and took in everything in his sight.

'A tree some way off, heather obviously, some sheep in the distance and a wall running between the moor and the pasture.'

Margaret turned him in the opposite direction.

'And now?'

Jay looked hard and replied much more quickly this time. 'More heather, more sheep, another tree and two more dry stone walls'.

'Very good,' said Margaret as if complimenting a pupil in a classroom. 'So what do you find interesting about your rock now?'

Jay thought for a moment. What could she mean? He looked back at his rock and then out again across the moor. What was so special about his boulder? Suddenly it hit him.

'All the walls around here are made of gritstone,' he said almost breathlessly, 'but this is limestone. It shouldn't be here, someone must have brought it here for a reason.'

Margaret smiled, taking great delight in the fact that Jay had noticed the anomaly. He returned to his rock and ran his hand over it.

'It seems very smooth and there are these two indentations on the top.'

'Excellent. Quite the detective!'

Jay smiled. He felt proud that he had managed to answer her question, but was struggling with the significance of his find. He looked around as if hoping to find another clue now that he had found the first. Nothing obvious, but then again he did not expect obvious now. He started to look around in the heather to see if there might be anything else hidden from view.

Within a very short space of time, his hands felt something else hard below the cover. He quickly separated the undergrowth and to his surprise found another stone, almost identical to the first. Limestone, with two indentations on the upper surface. He looked over at Margaret.

'What are they?'

Instead of answering his question, she asked one of her own.

'Are there any more?'

Jay moved again through the heather on his hands and knees parting the plants in such a way that it almost looked as if he was swimming. He found another and then another. Each time, the stones were about the same size, set into the earth so that they didn't move and with the two dents on the top.

'Notice anything about the ones you have found?' said Margaret, obviously trying to give him a clue about what he had discovered. Jay looked up to survey the stones. All the same type of rock, all the same size and shape, but he felt sure that was not what she meant.

'They're laid out in a semicircle!' he exclaimed.

Margaret smiled. 'Perhaps not just a semicircle,' she said, again trying to lead Jay to further discoveries.

Picking up on this immediately, he quickly moved through the heather and started to unearth more stones. After a few minutes he looked back at his handiwork. There were now twelve stones laid out in a perfect circle. Margaret was standing in the middle and seemed to have a look of complete contentment on her face. Jay stared at her.

The early morning sun was silhouetting her shape and shining through her hair, making it almost alive with the most amazing colours, and she seemed to radiate an aura that he could not describe or explain. She seemed almost not to notice him as he stood and gazed at her, marvelling at the look of total joy on her face.

Something now caught his attention. She seemed different but he could not immediately put his finger on what it was. It had nothing to do with the almost saintly look that she had taken on; it was something more basic than that. She's taller now, thought Jay to himself, but how can that be? He walked quietly over to her, giving her the same reverence that he would have given if he had been walking into a church. Oblivious to his movements, Jay stooped at her feet and saw that she was standing on another stone, the thirteenth stone of the circle. He stood back, not wanting to break the spell that she was under. Suddenly she spoke.

'We were meant to find this circle together,' she said in hushed tones. 'Your fate and mine are intertwined; your quest is crossed with my destiny.'

Jay just looked at her. He had absolutely no idea what she was talking about.

'What does this all mean?' he said, desperately wanting to understand what was going on. He knew he was part of something very special, but had no idea what it was.

Margaret looked down from her vantage point and put her hand out to touch his shoulder. It was as if someone had connected him to the mains. He felt an unearthly charge run straight through his body from his shoulder to his feet and return up the entire length of his backbone. He felt more alive than he had ever felt in his life. Colours seemed brighter, the sky seemed clearer and he could see for miles. The birdsong seemed louder and sweeter than he had ever experienced before and he felt as strong as an ox.

Yet still he had no answers. Margaret stepped down from her rock and the feeling subsided. He looked into her face and just knew she was special. Why and how he could not say, but there was no doubt in his mind that Margaret was no ordinary woman.

'I cannot lead you any further,' said Margaret as she started to walk around the twelve stones making up the outer circle. 'It is now up to you to discover the rest of the puzzle and for you to decide what to do with the knowledge'.

Jay had a thousand questions running through his mind but before he managed to blurt out the first one Margaret held up her hand as if to stop him.

'I cannot answer any of your questions,' she said. 'Your quest is your own and I have been able to guide you in the right direction, as your intentions are worthy. However, from here you must make your own future'.

Jay still did not understand. He needed to know what to do next. In an attempt to convince Margaret to help further he jumped up on to the stone next to the one she was now standing on. He looked deep in to her eyes and said, 'What must I do now?'

Margaret turned and began to walk the circumference of the circle. 'Walk with me, but in the opposite direction.'

Jay did not question her, but turned on his heels and started to walk away from Margaret. He concentrated on his feet so that he did not stumble as he made his way from stone to stone through the heather, which seemed to grasp at his ankles. When he had reached the centre point on the opposite side he stopped and looked up.

Margaret had gone!

***

Chapter 10

Chloe awoke and immediately felt that her pillow was damp. She reached for the light, not knowing what the time was because the thick curtains were still drawn and they kept out every ray of sunshine.

The clock said it was nearly 9 o'clock. She was still feeling tired so she lay back down. Not only was her pillow wet, but it was cold as well. She turned to investigate and immediately felt an involuntary scream leave her throat. Maggie came running up the stairs and burst in to her room. 'Whatever is the matter?' she gasped, fighting for breath between her rapid ascent of the stairs and her concern for Chloe.

'My pillow,' she sobbed, 'look at my pillow.' Maggie flicked on the light and saw that the pillow was soaked with blood.

'Don't worry,' she said reassuringly. 'You've just had a nasty nose bleed during the night.'

Chloe had become used to nose bleeds over the last few months. It seemed that they had been coming more regularly than before and each time they seemed to get worse. But this was the first time that she remembered waking up to find her pillow soaked though and it scared her.

She held out her arms to Maggie who bent down and hugged her close, as she had done to Chloe's mother not 24 hours before. She cradled the young-ster for some time until she seemed to have calmed down.

'Nothing to worry about,' Maggie kept reassuring her, but deep in her heart Chloe knew things were not right.

Maggie scooped her up in her arms and carried her out of the room. 'I'll make you comfortable on the sofa and then come back to change your bedding,' she said in a very matter of fact way that was meant to put Chloe's mind at rest.

Not wanting to put Maggie at risk going down the stairs, Chloe insisted on walking down herself, much against Maggie's protestations. However, as soon as her feet touched the floor she knew something was wrong. She seemed to have no strength at all and held on to the handrail for support. She was determined not to alarm Maggie so she set off down the stairs on her own.

When she was almost at the bottom she turned to speak to Maggie and then everything went black.

She opened her eyes and was looking into the tear-stained face of her mother.

'You had us so worried,' said Kathy, trying to sound completely under control in the way that mothers are supposed to do in such circumstances.

'You blacked-out coming down the stairs,' said Maggie, who was now coming into focus behind Kathy. 'I was so scared. I didn't know if you had banged your head or not so I called an ambulance and then your mother.'

Maggie looked so worried that Chloe felt sure she was blaming herself for the fall.

'It's not your fault,' she said reassuringly. 'I was determined to walk down the stairs on my own. I guess I didn't realise just how weak I was.'

Just at that moment a doctor came in to the room. 'So,' he said, sitting on the side of the bed, 'you thought you would give us all a scare, huh?'

Chloe smiled. She was certainly feeling okay now. She felt so silly being in a hospital bed surrounded by all these people.

'I'm fine. Can I go home now?'

The doctor frowned. 'I'm afraid not,' he said,

sounding very serious. 'It's normal to keep anyone in overnight who has possibly banged their head, so I suggest you get comfortable. We will keep an eye on you until tomorrow and if all is well you can go home then.'

Chloe's smile left her face in an instant. 'No!' she cried almost plaintively. 'Please let me go home, or back to Maggie's. It really wasn't her fault, Mum – don't blame her.'

Kathy smiled back at her daughter. 'Don't worry,' she said quietly, 'I don't blame Maggie. She's been an absolute wonder over these last few days and if she's prepared to have you back tomorrow I promise you can stay a couple more days while I get a few things done at home.'

Chloe beamed with happiness and held her hand out to Maggie who was now sitting on the side of the bed, grinning almost as much as Chloe.

'Next time, young lady, you do as I say so that we avoid any more flashing blue lights! You scared me half to death you did.'

Chloe looked deep into Maggie's eyes. 'I'm really and truly sorry. I hope you can forgive me.'

'Nothing to forgive,' replied Maggie. 'Let's just try and take things a little more slowly in future.'

The doctor came back in to the room with the X-rays and slipped them into place on the light box. 'Nothing appears to be broken,' he said as he squinted at the black and white images of Chloe's skull. 'Count yourself lucky this time.' He smiled at the assembled throng and then left, promising to check back in on her later.

'Where's Jay?' asked Chloe, all of a sudden remembering that she had not seen him.

'He went out for a walk early this morning and he hadn't returned by the time you gave us all a scare. But don't worry, Seth will let him know what has happened and I will bring him with me tomorrow when I come to pick you up.'

Chapter 11

Jay opened the door to the farm kitchen. Ben met him with a customary bark and bounded across to be rewarded with pats and hugs.

'I'm home!' he shouted, expecting to hear Maggie's voice, or at least Chloe's coming from the lounge.

Nothing. He slid off his shoes and walked across the floor. He looked back to see that he was leaving almost perfect footprints on the tiles, as the wet grass had soaked right through his shoes and made his socks quite sodden.

He bent down to peel them off and Ben took this as a sign to leap on him and knock him off his feet. The two of them rolled around the floor with Ben barking and jumping over Jay as he tried in vain to get up. This was a game that Ben was a master of. Jay was laughing so much that he was almost crying and Ben was licking his face and bouncing over him to keep him off guard.

Eventually Jay made it to his feet, ran to the stairs and then up to his bedroom. He carefully laid his socks over the radiator and found some clean dry ones before sitting on the side of his bed to put them on. He looked up and his heart almost stopped. He was staring straight at Chloe's pillow.

He sprang across the room and looked more closely. There was no doubt that it was blood. He bolted downstairs and ran from room to room shouting to anyone that might have heard him. Again nothing. He ran into the kitchen and saw a note on the table with his name on it. He ripped it open, being just careful enough not to tear its precious contents.

Dear Jay – Don't panic. Your sister woke up with a nose bleed and tripped as she was coming down the stairs. She may have banged her head so Maggie and your Mum have taken her to hospital as a precaution. I'm sure there is nothing to worry about, so try not to. Sorry I wasn't here when you got back, but I had to finish some dry stone walling in the high meadow. Maggie will be back soon. Seth.

Jay's heart was racing just a little slower now.

It had only been a nose bleed. She'd had a lot of them recently but this one seemed the worst so far. Should he call the hospital? Where *was* the hospital? Should he be there to help? So many questions raced through his mind. He looked around the kitchen as if looking for an answer and it came in the form of Ben laying his head in Jay's lap as if to say, 'Don't worry, it will be all right.'

It is amazing the soothing effect an animal can have on a human.

At that moment he heard a car pulling into the yard and Jay ran out to see who it was. It was Maggie. He rushed over to her and she threw her arms around him. Without warning he started to cry and Maggie held him close until the tears had stopped.

'There, there,' she said, wiping his cheeks with the sleeve of her blouse. 'Nothing to worry about. Chloe is fine. She has to stay in overnight as a precaution, but you and I will go and pick her up tomorrow and your mother has said that the two of you can stay a little longer if you would like to.'

Jay hugged her even harder. 'Thanks Maggie,' he whispered into her warm sweater and the two of them walked slowly across the yard and back into the kitchen, arms firmly around each other for comfort.

That evening, after they had eaten their tea, Jay pestered Maggie to tell him anything and everything she knew about The Hill Folk. Maggie told story after story and Jay listened intently, hoping that he might glean a useful piece of information about the elusive Midnight Rose. Despite Maggie regaling him with tales from the area for over an hour, Jay learned nothing new that would help him with his quest.

'What time will we be picking Chloe up tomorrow?'

'About four o'clock,' said Maggie, picking up the two hot chocolate mugs that were now standing empty on the coffee table. 'Why do you ask?'

Jay wasn't sure how to answer. Should he tell her about today's meeting with Margaret and about the stone circle that he had uncovered? Sometimes he felt it would be OK to confess what he was up to and other times he felt it best to just keep quiet until he had found what he was looking for.

'I suppose you'll want to be up early and across the moor again,' said Maggie in her matter of fact manner. 'Just be sure you're back in plenty of time to go and pick up your sister. We'll need to be leaving by three to be in plenty of time, so you be sure to wear your watch.'

Jay just looked at her. He was more certain than ever that she was psychic and knew what he was going to do next before he knew himself.

'Off to bed with you now. You've a big day ahead of you tomorrow.'

Jay kissed her on the cheek, patted Ben who was lying by the fireplace, and made his way up the stairs. He changed into his pyjamas and brushed his teeth before sliding into his wonderfully warm bed. He decided not to read any more of the local history books this evening and as soon as his head hit the pillow he drifted off into a deep sleep.

'Often things are much closer than you think.' The voice was a familiar one. It was Margaret.

'What do you mean?'

'I cannot lead you any further.'

She was standing on the stone at the centre of the circle with her arms outstretched and she was slowly turning.

'Where do I need to look next?' he asked with a real urgency in his voice.

'Things are much closer than you think.'

Jay sat up suddenly in his bed. His breathing was shallow and fast and he had sweat on his brow. He had been dreaming, but somehow it seemed more than a dream. Certainly it all seemed more real than any dream he had ever dreamt before.

He now knew where he must go first thing in the morning.

Chapter 12

Maggie was cooking breakfast when Jay came down to the kitchen. He had slept a deep and restful sleep after waking from his dream. It was as though his whole body had shut down from sheer relief after the realisation of what he must do next.

It was of no surprise that Maggie was already up ahead of him. He felt quite sure that if he had come down in the middle of the night she would have been standing in the kitchen cooking breakfast.

Jay sat down at the table and Ben lay across his feet as he always did, hoping that something would end up on the floor. As usual, it didn't. Still, he lived in hope and it never seemed to change his demeanour. That was the amazing thing about dogs: no matter what happens, they always come back wagging their tails having forgiven or forgotten whatever may have upset them ten minutes before. Wouldn't the world benefit from people having that same ability? he thought to himself as Maggie put three rashers of bacon on his plate next to his two eggs.

He slowly cut up and ate what had been put before him while Maggie busied herself around the kitchen. They didn't speak at all as he feasted and his mind was already up on the moor. He finished his breakfast and took his plate over to the sink.

'Just leave it, dear,' said Maggie as he began to wash it under the running water. 'I know that you want to get out and back on to the hill, so off you go. Just be sure to be back in time to go and pick up your sister. Have you got your watch?'

Jay held up his wrist and pulled back his shirt-sleeve to show that he had indeed got the watch on, as there was no way he was going to miss picking up Chloe. Maggie smiled and wished him luck.

'I hope you find what you're looking for today,' she shouted after him as he raced through the yard and out of the back gate.

Not as much as I do, he thought as he ran along the path, over the first stile and out across the field. Within minutes he was back on familiar ground, running through the damp grass, scaring the sheep who ran aimlessly in all directions, and across to the high pasture. Standing on top of the wall he looked back down the valley towards the farm. He couldn't see the building, but he could make out the smoke rising from the chimneys. He turned and clambered down again and made his way across to the margins of the heather. This time he didn't need to stop and work out where the track was that allowed him to make his way through the coarse undergrowth. He ran straight to it and quickly pushed his way along to where he had brushed back the foliage yesterday to expose the ring of stones.

There it all was, just as he had left it yesterday. He looked around expecting to see Margaret, but she was nowhere in sight. He remembered how she had just appeared on previous visits and felt sure that she would suddenly be standing behind him. He made his way around the circle, looking at every stone in turn to see if there was a visible clue, just a hint of what he should do next or where he should go.

Nothing. All the stones looked identical and had no markings at all save the two dents on the top.

Frustrated, he sat down on the final stone and looked back at where he had begun. There had to be something. He was obviously just not looking hard enough. He spun around and looked in towards the centre of the ring. Suddenly the rock seemed incredibly comfortable and he realised in an instant that the stones were shaped to fit like the seat of a chair.

These were obviously for people to sit on so that everyone could look into the centre of the arena, like the Knights of the Round Table, everyone equal, except for the stone in the centre. This was the stone that Margaret had been standing on yesterday when she seemed to drift away to a different place and where she had been standing in his dream last night. He leaped to his feet and ran to the middle of the circle. He dropped to his knees and ran his hands over the surface of the rock.

It seemed just like the others; smooth to the touch, but had no depressions on it. This was no sitting place. This was where the leader must have stood, where the most revered of the council would have listened and judged and dispensed their wisdom.

Jay's head was swimming. It was almost as if he could feel a power emanating from the stone, a strange natural force that made the hairs on the back of his neck stand up. He realised that his fingers were now inadvertently tracing small lines along the surface. They were well-worn and he had no idea whether they were man-made or just ancient crevasses in the natural fabric of the stone.

He remembered a trick he had seen on television when an archaeologist was trying to read hieroglyphics on an old Egyptian tomb. They had covered the area with sand and then gently blown it off from the side so that it filled the lines and made a pattern that was easily visible.

He had no sand, but picked up a handful of peat. It was dry and should do the trick, he thought to himself. Gently he rolled the peat between his fingers so that it was a fine dust. He then carefully covered the whole of the stone's surface until no rock was showing. He lowered his head so that his mouth was level with the stone and gently started to blow.

The peat dust moved under the force of his breath, but did not clear to leave a picture as he had hoped. He decided to try again. This time as he blew, a breeze appeared as if from nowhere and the heather began to rustle all around him. He could feel the wind in his hair and as he looked at the stone the dust seemed to be swept to one side as if someone had run a brush across it.

Trembling, he slowly stood up and looked down on the rock. His heart missed a beat as he realised that before him, without a shadow of a doubt, was the picture of a flower. Not just any flower – it was a rose.

He had found The Midnight Rose!

Chapter 13

All the way down off the moor Jay ran as if he had wings on his feet. He couldn't stop smiling and on more than one occasion he scattered the sheep to the four corners of the field by screaming at the top of his voice. He had no idea what he was screaming or even why; it just seemed the thing to do. He had found The Midnight Rose.

'Just wait until I tell Chloe,' he thought as he leaped from the top of the stile and felt as if he was flying.

Nothing could spoil his day now. He raced through the high meadow and down towards the farm, stopping only to shout Hello to a blackbird that was sitting in a tree watching him in sheer amazement.

As he got within sight of the yard, he saw

Maggie hanging some washing out and he shouted to her, waving his arms. She opened the back gate and Ben came sprinting across the field, leaping on Jay and knocking him totally backwards into a tuft of tall cotton grass and then he administered his usual tongue washing.

Ben could sense Jay's good mood and decided to take advantage of it. They wrestled to and fro in the grass with Ben barking and Jay laughing and Maggie eventually came across to see what all the noise was about.

'My my, you look happy,' she said looking down at the tangled mass of boy and dog. 'I assume you had a profitable morning up on the moor?'

'The best,' Jay replied. 'Maggie, it was unbelievable.'

'Well, you will have to tell me all about it in the car,' she said. 'You need to go and get changed as we have to leave in about ten minutes.'

'I'll be ready,' shouted Jay as he leapt to his feet, patted Ben and ran inside, only stopping long enough to flick his damp shoes into the corner of the kitchen porch before tearing up the stairs, singing.

Maggie smiled one of her knowing smiles. By the time she had put away her laundry basket and changed her shoes, Jay was back downstairs, washed (well, sort of), hair combed (as far as he was concerned, it was), and raring to go. He chivvied Maggie along, much to her amusement, and the two climbed into Maggie's car.

'Your mother is going to meet us there,' said Maggie as they turned into Cob Lane. 'She was hoping to have a quick word with the doctor before we get there and then help Chloe get ready. She was taking her a change of clothes and a bite to eat.'

Jay was listening, but was so excited at the thought of telling his sister all about his find that he really didn't hear what Maggie was saying.

'So what exactly happened up there on the moor today?' asked Maggie when she thought she had caught his attention.

'If I tell you, will you keep it a secret?' Jay hoped that the answer was Yes, but knew he would tell her anyway.

'If that's what you want,' replied Maggie solemnly.

Jay then proceeded to tell her all about his meetings with Margaret, how they had uncovered the stone circle, how he had dreamed that he should go to the centre stone and how he had found The Midnight Rose.

Maggie listened to his story as they drove down the road, never stopping to ask questions, just listening to the excited boy telling his tale. Eventually, when he stopped talking, Maggie turned to look at him.

'That is absolutely wonderful, Jay. So what are you going to do now?'

Then, and only then, did Jay stop to think about what indeed he should do now. He was so excited about finding The Midnight Rose that he had never stopped to think about what it meant, what he should do now and how it might help Chloe.

Just when he thought nothing could spoil his day, he was completely floored by Maggie's simple question. Jay gazed out of the window for what seemed the longest time while he tried to come up with a sensible answer. Maggie sensed his dilemma and turned on the radio to help overcome the awkward silence and to give Jay time to think.

At the end of the song that was playing, the announcer said that it was time to hand over to the news team, but he would be back in three minutes with the answer to today's quiz. Jay was still thinking about what his discovery really meant when the newsreader started his rundown of the main global news stories of the day. At the end he said: 'And to finish on a lighter note, be sure to keep your windows and doors tightly locked tonight as we have an unusual alignment of four planets this evening. People all over the country are predicting everything from the end of the world to the second coming of Jesus Christ. No doubt there will be more than the usual smattering of weirdos on the streets this evening,' he chuckled, 'but for those of you interested in seeing a once-in-a-lifetime event, you will be able to see the planets coming into alignment from about 11 o'clock tonight. Depending where you are in the country you will need to look slightly to the east of north and about 40 degrees up from the horizon. If the sky is favourable and there aren't too many clouds, it should be a spectacular sight. It only comes around about once every one hundred years.'

With that the news finished and the station returned to music. Maggie said nothing, but she did look straight at Jay and smiled. Before he could speak he found they were pulling into the hospital car park and his thoughts were back on Chloe.

'Just through these doors in front of us,' said Maggie, 'and then down the corridor to the left. Chloe is in room 24.'

Jay didn't stop to see if Maggie was following him. He charged across the car park and into the building. He slowed down, realising where he was and not wanting to cause any accidents, even though this was the perfect place to have them if you had to have them at all, he smiled to himself.

He saw the numbers on the doors and started to follow them. 16, 18, 20 – not much further, he told himself but then he stopped dead in his tracks.

He was sure that he heard his mother's voice.

'Are you absolutely certain?' said his mother, her voice quaking as she spoke.

'I wish I could tell you that I was wrong,' came the reply. 'I wish I could tell you that there was even the chance that I was wrong, but I'm afraid there isn't. We contacted Leeds after you had left yesterday, given the history that you had supplied us with, and at their suggestion we ran some more tests. The results came back exactly as we feared they would. The diagnosis backs up what Leeds had found previously. I'm really sorry.'

Jay stood motionless. They were talking about his sister, his only sister.

'So what exactly are you telling me?' he heard his mother ask, weaker than he had ever heard her sound before.

'I'm afraid we are saying that it is so advanced there is nothing that can be done for her. I'm sorry to have to tell you ... she has only a few weeks to live, perhaps a couple of months at the most.'

Jay's blood ran cold. This could not be happening. They could not be talking about Chloe, about his sister. He wanted to cry, but he was so numb that he couldn't do anything. He felt a hand on his shoulder and he looked around slowly, as if in a trance. It was Maggie. She had heard everything. She slowly bent down and knelt in front of Jay.

'Your mother doesn't know that we have heard this conversation,' she began, 'and we are going to have to let her deal with this in her own way. You are going to have to be more grown up than you have ever had to be in your short life, and pretend you heard nothing. You cannot say anything to your mother and you certainly cannot say anything to Chloe. Do you understand?'

Jay nodded.

'We need to go in now to see Chloe and we have to act normally. It's going to be the hardest thing you will ever have to do in your life, but you need to do it for Chloe'.

Jay nodded again. 'I don't know if I can do it,' he whispered, his voice having all but disappeared.

'You can,' said Maggie forcefully, 'and you will!'

She pulled him to her and they stayed locked together for what seemed like an age. As they hugged, Jay felt a strength surge into his body. He was a boy on a quest again and he knew he had been given a challenge that he must rise to. He released Maggie, turned and opened the door to room 24 to find Chloe sitting on the edge of the bed. She smiled as she saw who it was coming in and Jay ran across and threw his arms around her.

Chloe looked pale, but apart from that she

seemed her normal self.

'Can we go home now?' she asked as Maggie entered the room.

'Just as soon as your mother gets back.'

It was a few minutes before Kathy appeared and when she did, it was obvious to Maggie that she had been crying and had washed her face in an effort to look respectable.

'Ready to go?' she asked.

That was a pointless question if ever there was one! Chloe slipped off the bed and collected the small bundle of pyjamas that she had been wearing when she had been admitted yesterday. She was tightly gripping Kathy's hand as they made their way along the corridor to the exit and Jay followed close behind holding Maggie's.

They walked over to where the cars were parked – by coincidence right next to each other – and then Kathy hugged Chloe again.

'Are you sure you don't want to come straight home?' she enquired.

'Yes,' said Chloe, but not wanting to sound too ungrateful she added, 'if you're sure you don't mind?' She really liked it over at Maggie's farm and wanted to stay there a little longer.

'Are you sure *you* don't mind?' asked Kathy looking at Maggie.

'It would be a pleasure,' she beamed. 'Besides,

you may want a little time to yourself right now.'

Kathy wasn't sure why Maggie had said this, but she was not going to argue; she felt totally drained by the news that the doctor had given her. 'Why don't you come over later and we'll chat over a hot chocolate?'

Kathy smiled. 'That sounds really good.'

'No rush,' said Maggie. 'Whenever you feel like it, we'll be there.'

With that Maggie opened her car door and the kids climbed into the back. They all waved to Kathy as the Land Rover pulled out of the car park and started along the road towards home. They did not see Kathy get into her car and collapse in a flood of tears, her arms crossed on top of the steering wheel. It was better that they hadn't.

No one spoke on the journey back to the farm, but Jay and Chloe sat close to each other, hand in hand. They didn't need to speak. Chloe felt safe back with her brother and Jay's mind was already working on a plan to save his sister.

Chapter 14

As soon as they arrived home, Maggie made sure Chloe was comfortable in front of the television and then asked Jay to help her in the kitchen. When they were out of earshot, she turned to Jay.

'I am so proud of you,' she said, with tears visible in her eyes. 'Chloe and your mother really need your strength now, even if they don't realise it. You can help them both through this, but it will be hard. Remember, you still cannot tell Chloe about what you heard, you must leave that to your mother.'

Jay nodded his understanding and agreement.

'Now get yourself back in there and keep your sister company.'

Maggie busied herself with making tea. She

wanted this to be extra special, so she whipped up a batch of chocolate chip cookies while she cooked their favourite: nuggets and chips.

'A feast fit for a king,' she declared as she carried the food in on a tray. This was a rare treat, as they were not normally allowed to eat in the lounge. Jay tucked into his like a man possessed. He had not had time to eat any lunch when he had come down from the moor, but had been too excited to notice. He was now ravenous and tucked in with great gusto. Chloe, however, seemed to be just picking at her food.

'I'm really sorry, Maggie,' she said most apologetically, 'but I just don't feel hungry.'

'Just eat what you can,' said Maggie reassuringly. 'You need to keep your strength up'.

After they had eaten, they played numerous card games, which was a great way of keeping everyone occupied and helped to keep their minds off the underlying concern.

By 9:30 Chloe was really starting to fade, so Maggie suggested they head off to bed and she would bring them a hot drink in their bedroom. Jay and Chloe grudgingly agreed and they said their goodnights to Ben as they made their way to the foot of the stairs.

'Follow your sister up,' instructed Maggie, not wanting to see her tumble down the stairs again.

Like a royal bodyguard Jay moved in close behind Chloe – so close, in fact, that she turned around and crossly told him to give her some space. Jay smiled, that was more like the Chloe he loved!

They quickly washed and changed and slid into their respective beds. No sooner had they settled down than Maggie appeared with two steaming hot mugs of chocolate. Just as she had handed one to Chloe, she heard the doorbell downstairs.

'Here you go,' she said, handing the second mug to Jay. 'That will be your mother. I'll go and let her in. You get comfy and she'll come up and see you in a little while.'

Maggie shut the door behind her so that she and Kathy could have some privacy, and the children heard her descending the stairs.

'You really had us all worried,' said Jay, this being the first time he had been alone with his sister since the accident.

'Sorry,' said Chloe. 'I didn't do it on purpose, you know.'

'I know you didn't,' he replied. 'I'm just glad you're okay.'

Chloe looked at him over the top of her warm mug. She liked the caring side of Jay; it made her feel warm inside, just like the hot chocolate.

Downstairs Maggie was making two more mugs

and Ben, who was his usual cheery self, was making Kathy welcome in the lounge. He had an amazing ability to greet everyone with the same selfless affection that he had when greeting Maggie. He was lying across Kathy's feet when Maggie entered with the tray of drinks and the few remaining biscuits that Jay had not vacuumed down at teatime.

Maggie had a knack of making everyone feel at home and soon Kathy found she was opening her heart to her. Years of concerns and fears were flowing out of her and she seemed unable to stop. Maggie sat and listened, not saying anything. There was nothing to say. Kathy had endured more pain than most people would ever encounter in a lifetime and she just needed someone to unload to. Eventually she came to a pause.

'I'm really sorry,' she said, looking down into her now cold chocolate. 'You don't need to hear all my problems, particularly when you have been so kind.'

'Don't be silly,' replied Maggie, 'that's what I'm here for.' She looked at her watch. 'We'd better go up so that you can say goodnight to the children. We've been down here for over an hour.'

The time had just flown by and even though Kathy was sure they would be asleep by now, she wanted to go up and kiss them goodnight. Creeping quietly up the stairs, Maggie led the way to their bedroom. She knew just how to open the door without it creaking, as the last thing she wanted to do was wake Chloe.

As it happened, she needn't have worried. The children were gone.

Chapter 15

Kathy screamed. Was there anything else that could happen? Where were her children? What had happened to them?

Maggie grabbed her by the shoulders. 'Don't worry,' she said quietly, 'I think I know where they are. Follow me and I'll explain on the way.'

Maggie stopped long enough in the kitchen to write a note for Seth explaining where they had gone and then she made for the back door. 'Put these on,' she said, handing Kathy a pair of Wellington boots, 'you'll need them.'

Maggie grabbed a torch and started off across the yard with Kathy in close pursuit. As they made their way carefully across the field, Maggie explained to Kathy about Jay's 'quest' and how he had unearthed the stone circle on the moor. She explained how Jay was sure that it had some magical healing power and that she was sure they would find them there. Kathy was beside herself with worry but went along, trusting that Maggie knew what she was doing.

Chloe was tired, so tired. She was trying to keep walking, but she seemed to have no strength left.

'Come on, Chloe,' implored Jay. 'It really isn't much further. I know you can do it.' He was half supporting, half carrying her by the time they reached the heather line.

'I need to rest,' she said, 'and I can't see where I'm going.'

As she spoke, the clouds slipped away from the face of the moon and the landscape was illuminated with a magical glow. The heather was lit by an eerie bluey yellow tint and everything was now visible to the children.

'We have to keep going,' said Jay as he slid his arm under her shoulder to ensure she didn't just give up and sit down. He was like a man possessed. He just knew in his heart that if he could get her to the stone circle, everything would be OK. They stumbled along the narrow path through the heather, but somehow, tonight it seemed that the coarse fronds were not clawing at their ankles. The path seemed wider, wide enough for Jay to walk alongside his sister to help her the last few hundred yards.

Kathy and Maggie were making ground quickly on the children now, as they could move much faster than Chloe. Maggie looked up and she saw a movement in the moonlight.

'There they are!' she shouted, pointing into the distance so that Kathy could get a bearing on the children.

With renewed energy Kathy launched herself along the path that would eventually lead her to the stone circle, although she had no way of knowing that.

The children arrived at the arena and Jay looked around, expecting to see something, but not knowing exactly what. He looked skywards and saw the planets that the man on the radio had been talking about. They were almost in line now and really were quite beautiful. However, that was purely by-the-by. He had brought his sister there to be healed by The Midnight Rose and he was not sure what he should do next.

'Chloe, Jay!'

It was Kathy. She was now only a few yards down the path and she stopped to look at them. 'What on earth do you think you are doing? You should be in bed, not out here on the moor. Jay, what were you thinking – dragging your sister out in the middle of the night? Don't you know how sick she is?' Kathy's voice was a mixture of anguish and concern.

'That is exactly why he has brought her here.'

Jay spun around to see who had just spoken. It was Margaret. She was standing in the centre of the circle, her arms outstretched with the moon's rays glinting off her beautiful robes.

Kathy stood there dumbfounded. Jay made to enter the circle, but Margaret raised her hand and said: 'Not you, Jay. You must stay where you are. It is Chloe who must join me in the circle.'

Kathy had regained her composure now and strode forward, putting her hands on Chloe's shoulders.

'You are not going anywhere, Chloe,' she said putting her arms around her daughter to protect her. 'I don't know who you are, or what you think you're doing, but I am not letting you anywhere near my daughter.'

'Let her enter the circle, Kathy.'

This time it was a man's voice. Kathy's jaw dropped. From behind Margaret came a man who had obviously been sitting on one of the stones.

'Hello Kathy, don't be afraid.'

Kathy tried to speak but couldn't.

'Peter?' she stammered. 'Is that really you?'

Kathy's husband stepped from Margaret's shadow and stood by her in the centre of the circle.

'Don't be afraid,' he repeated calmly.

'Dad?' croaked Jay.

'I'm proud of you, son. You have worked hard to help your sister and now you have brought her to a place where she can be free of her ills.'

'Dad – are you for real?' said Chloe, almost afraid that this was all a dream.

'Yes, pumpkin,' he said with a smile. 'It really is me.'

Kathy fell to her knees and Jay ran over to help her. Margaret then spoke again.

'Jay helped me to find and recover the stone circle and for that I shall be forever in his debt. We can help Chloe, Kathy, but it is going to take your trust and understanding.'

'Listen to her, Kathy,' said Peter, who had now moved to the front of the circle near to Chloe.

'We cannot cure her in this world,' explained Margaret, 'but if she steps into the circle she will enter a place where time and illness have no meaning. Chloe will live forever and never be troubled by her earthbound problems. She will stay with her father and together they will watch over you both. They will not be bound by the limitations of time and state, as you are in your world, but will be free to travel wherever their hearts desire. She will be happy forever.'

Kathy just stared. She had no idea what to say. She was looking at her husband for the first time since the day she had buried him and knew that if she truly was awake, she was in the middle of a miracle.

'Let her go, mum,' said Jay.

He was walking over to his mother and without a further word he gently took her arms from around Chloe. 'You know this is the right thing to do. I heard the conversation with the doctor, mum. This is her only chance.'

Kathy stood motionless. It is incredible how children often deal with the unexpected so much better than their parents and this was one such occasion.

Jay took his sister's hand and he led her to the side of the stones.

'I love you, Chloe,' he said and gently kissed her on the forehead. Without a word, Chloe turned, blew a kiss to her mother and then stepped into the circle. As she entered, a bright beam of light illuminated her from the sky.

Jay looked up. The planets were now aligned and a strong shaft of pale pink light cut through the sky like a spotlight, shining directly on Chloe.

She looked radiant. The colour was back in her

cheeks as she ran into her father's arms. Kathy wasn't crying, but tears were rolling down her cheeks.

'Do not be afraid or concerned,' said Margaret. 'I have promised you that she will now be well and that she will live forever without the worries of her mortal body. Form and time will no longer dictate her life.'

Jay was not sure what she meant by that, but before he could ask, his sister turned and stepped forward.

'Remember me?' she said.

Jay looked at her face; it was the girl from the train.

'I am an old soul,' she said, 'one of The Hill Folk.'

Jay looked again. Before him was now standing the girl who had pulled him from the river.

His mind was racing. He didn't understand. Could it be that it was his own sister who had brought about the events culminating in them all standing there beside the stone circle that night? How could that be? He had a thousand questions, but just looking at his sister's face he knew that he should not ask them.

He just knew that he should accept what was happening before him and be happy for Chloe. She may be heading out of his world, but she would be with him forever, this he knew. Here she would be well. If she stayed with him, her life would be short.

He looked from Chloe to his father and then to his mother. She had still not said a word. Jay took his mother's hand in his and simply said, 'Let her go, mum.'

Kathy's tears had dried. She had an expression of pure joy on her face. 'Look after her, Peter,' she said running her hand through Jay's hair. 'Visit us when you can.'

'We will always be with you,' he said and she knew that he was telling the truth. 'You may not recognise us, but you will know we are there.'

The beam of moonlight was beginning to fade.

'We must leave you now,' said Margaret. 'As the planets are moving, so must we. Do not grieve for Peter and Chloe – they are together again and free of hurt. Be proud of your son, Kathy, and live each day for the joy that you can bring each other.'

The light was fading even more now and the three figures, standing hand in hand, side by side, slowly melted away into the shadows, leaving Kathy and Jay alone on the moor. Neither knew what to say to the other, so Jay turned and started to make his way down the path.

'Where's Maggie?' asked Kathy. She had completely lost track of her since she arrived at the circle.

'I've no idea,' said Jay. 'She must be back at the farm.'

Silently they made their way back through the heather, across the high meadow and down through the fields. As they walked they felt an overwhelming peace, but a sense of loss, knowing that they would not see Chloe again, or at least not as they had seen her earlier that day. The whole event had seemed incredible, a miracle that they had been part of.

Soon they were back at the farmyard and they made their way across to the kitchen door. The light was on in the kitchen so they knocked to attract Maggie's attention. The door opened.

'Can I help you?'

Before them stood a lady that they did not recognise.

'Is Maggie here?' asked Kathy, a little surprised to see the stranger in Maggie's kitchen. The stranger looked at them and quietly said, 'I think you had better come in.'

Kathy and Jay sat down at the table and the stranger pulled up a chair on the other side.

'You say you have come to see Maggie?' asked the stranger.

'That's right,' said Kathy. 'Is she here?'

'My name is Sarah,' said the stranger, 'and this is my house. I've lived here for 25 years and I can assure you that there is no Maggie.'

Jay and Kathy stared at each other. They looked around. This was the kitchen that they had been in only a few hours ago. Everything was exactly as they knew it. What was this woman talking about? Suddenly Jay grabbed his mother's arm.

'Look!' he shouted. 'Look at the pictures on the wall!'

Kathy turned and stared at the frames hanging over the worktop. 'Chloe!' she croaked, looking at the furthest most photograph.

'I'm sorry,' said Sarah. 'Did you say Chloe? That's a photo of me when I was about 10 or 11.'

Kathy's eyes moved on to the next picture. 'Peter...' she said, almost in a whisper as she saw the frame contained a photo of her husband.

'That's Seth,' explained Sarah. 'He was my grandfather and he lived here in this farm many years ago.'

'That is Maggie,' said Kathy, her head spinning as she now looked at the third photo.

'That's right,' said Sarah. 'Maggie was Seth's wife, my grandmother.'

Jay and Kathy were now holding hands on top of the table trying to take in everything that was happening.

Finally Kathy looked at the last photo. 'Margaret?' she asked.

'That's what some people called her when she was young. She preferred to be called Maggie, as she grew older. It's just a picture of Maggie when she was much younger and before she met Seth.

'She was very well known around these parts as being a member of The Hill Folk, but I doubt you will ever have heard of them. Margaret was her birth name, Margaret Rose Pendle, but the people around here knew her as Midnight Rose.'

Chapter 16

Jay and Kathy rose early that morning. Although they hardly said a word to each other as they hurried around the house getting ready, they both knew that they would visit the cemetery that day. It was strange; it was almost as if they were being summoned to attend rather than going to pay their respects.

On the way they stopped to pick up flowers. Kathy had always brought a bunch of white chrysanthemums when she had visited Peter's grave. They had been his favourite ever since she could remember and he had bought her a bouquet of white and yellow blooms the day before he had died. Kathy had kept them for weeks, not wanting to throw them out and it was Chloe who eventually put them in the bin. Today, however, she bought two bunches.

As they walked up the path between the headstones, Jay gently took his mother's hand in his own and smiled reassuringly at her. They made their way to their familiar spot, their shadows moving playfully over the close-cropped grass while the sun rose overhead. As always, Jay arrived first.

'Mum!' Jay was looking at the headstone with surprise etched all over his face.

Kathy caught up and allowed her gaze to follow his. Sitting in the two matching vases that they had bought after Chloe's departure were two pristine bunches of yellow and white Chrysanths. Surely these couldn't be the ones they had left last time? It had been two weeks since their last visit and the weather had not been great. Neither spoke, but they both looked from the flowers to each other and back to the flowers.

'I hope you don't mind,' came a voice from behind them.

Jay and Kathy turned to see where it had come from. There stood a strong, broad man with a kind but weatherworn face.

'I'm the caretaker here,' he said, leaning slightly to one side, his weight being taken on a long scythe that he had been using to trim the long grass around the cemetery.

'My daughter and I put the flowers there yesterday. She seems to have adopted your family; I hope you don't mind. Perhaps it is because she felt there had been no closure for the little girl, having heard that you never found the body after she went out on to the tops the day she disappeared. Don't know really, she has never said. She just asked if we could get some flowers yesterday when we were out shopping. She chose them herself and as soon as we got home she brought them out here.'

Jay and Kathy looked at the man, not knowing what to say.

'She asked me if we could make a special effort to always look after this plot. In fact, there she is now, over by the big oak tree. I'll call her over.'

Kathy was still standing with her two bunches of flowers, unable to say anything. Her mind was racing, but uncannily she felt a wave of calm sweeping over her.

The man waved his arm in the air towards his daughter to attract her attention.

'Maggie! Come over here will you?'

A chill ran down Kathy's spine.

'Thank you, Seth,' said Jay.

'You're welcome,' came the reply. 'Have we met before?'

***

Part Two
Elspeth's Canvas

Chapter 1

'You can't be serious!' Dave looked at his parents in total disbelief.

'Mum, Dad, give me a break! Not Grandma, anyone but Grandma.'

Dave lived a comfortable life, in a comfortable house in Congleton, Cheshire. He had lived there his entire life, 12 years to be exact. His was not an exciting life, but it suited him. His parents were both Accountants, which he tried to keep a secret from his friends. They left every morning to commute in to Manchester and he was expected to organise himself to get off to school on time, to get home again and start his homework so that it was all but finished by the time they reappeared about 7:30 in the evening. He didn't really see a great deal of them for that reason and he had developed an entirely independent life of which they knew nothing. Dave didn't really mind this, as so many of his friends had parents who 'cared' and, therefore, were always explaining where they were, what they were doing and who they were with. Dave had none of these issues to worry about and that was just fine by him.

His parents had known each other since they were at primary school. They had gone to secondary school together, attended the same university, went to work for the same firm, got married and still worked in the same office. This was a totally alien concept to most of Dave's friends who taunted him mercilessly on occasions, but despite all this, Dave still thought his parents were pretty cool. They also got to travel together on business when they had to go and audit the accounts of overseas subsidiaries of UK customers. Dave thought this was generally OK, as it was during school time and he stayed with his Uncle Pete, who was a bit wild for his parents liking, but at least he lived locally. This trip was going to be different. Not only was it during his upcoming summer break, but they were trying to line him up with his grandmother.

'Why can't I stay with Uncle Pete, like I

always do?'

'Because Uncle Pete is going to be away at the same time,' explained his mother, hoping that this in itself would be enough to bring an end to the discussion.

'What about Bob, then? Why can't I stay with him?'

Bob was Dave's best friend. They had started nursery school together and been in the same classes all through primary school, except for year five, when one of the overly intrusive teachers thought it would be a good idea if she broke up 'The Terrible Twins' for a while to see if they would concentrate a little harder in class.

'We are going to be away for ten days,' explained his father, 'and that is too long to put upon anyone but family. I'm sure you understand.'

All Dave understood was that this time his parents had gone way too far.

'There is no chance I am going to stay with Grandma. She lives in the middle of nowhere. She's a complete head case, everyone thinks she's totally crazy and I hardly know her!'

His father, Jasper, was secretly thinking that Dave actually had a number of valid points, but he wasn't going to let him get away with that outburst. He had been there before and didn't want to catch the rough end of Zoe's tongue again, thank you very much. She turned and looked at him and gave him a piercing stare as if she knew exactly what he was thinking. Jasper quickly looked away, hoping that would keep him out of trouble.

'That's not fair,' said his mother. 'Your Grandma may be a little, how shall I say, eccentric, but she certainly isn't crazy. I'm sure you will have a great time. She is a wonderful lady when you get to know her.'

'How come I overheard you two discussing ways of avoiding inviting her for Christmas this year, then? And if she is so great, why does she never come to stay? Answer me that. There is no way it is happening. End of story. End of discussion!'

Dave stormed out of the room and headed up the stairs. With a slam of his door he retreated into his private domain to stew.

'That went pretty well, all things considered,' said Jasper as he bent to pick up a few magazines which had been swept off the table in Dave's dramatic exit. He looked up, hoping to find Zoe's smiling face, amused by his sarcastic wit. How wrong could he have been? Zoe had a face like thunder and she was looking at him in the same way that she would look at something she had trodden in by mistake.

'If there was any choice in the matter, I certainly wouldn't be relying on my mother, but there isn't, so the least you can do is be supportive.'

'Sorry, dear.'

It was one of those moments where there is no alternative but to apologise and go with the flow. Secretly, Jasper quite liked her mother, he always had. Under his Accountant title and Accountant clothes there was a rebel trying to get out. He often looked at his brother, Pete, and wished that they could trade lives. Pete was a painter and decorator, seemed to have not a care in the world, was still single and spent his weekends drinking with his mates and riding his motorbike around the country. This was probably why Dave looked forward to staying with him when his parents went away. Elspeth, Zoe's mother, had always marched to the beat of her own drum. Her name was actually Molly but some years earlier she had decided to change it by deed poll and no one had ever really understood why. To be honest, no one had ever bothered to ask her.

Amongst a thousand other things, Zoe had never forgiven her for calling her Zoe. She would have preferred an ordinary name that would have fitted in much more easily with her desire for an ordinary life. She had often thought about changing her name when she was younger but to her, changing your name was even more unacceptable than living with one you didn't like, so she had just learned to live with it. Molly, or should I say Elspeth, really liked the name Zoe; in fact she liked most things that were a little unusual. She had suddenly become all 'New Age' when Zoe had gone off to university and she had moved from the security of her home to open a shop selling crystals, candles and herbal remedies in Lancashire. 'In Pendle Witch Country,' as she would proudly tell anyone who would listen, which was not very often.

Molly had married young and Zoe was born by the time she was twenty. By twenty-one she was alone, having realised that the man she had married was content to live a suburban life whereas she had a hankering to discover what the world had to offer. For the next few years she had bravely travelled around Africa and even more impressively had taken Zoe with her. Zoe had no recollection of this adventurous time, either because she had been too young, or because she had chosen to blank it out, as it was so out of keeping with the person she now was. Jasper often thought this was a great shame, as he loved to hear tales of when they lived with the Masai for a period and how they had learned to live off the land. He found it hard to believe looking at Zoe now, but he was happy with the way they were and thankful that he had a job that let him spend so much time with her.

Molly had eventually decided that she should move back to the UK when Zoe had reached four and a half so that she could start to get a 'proper' education, whatever that meant. Looking back on it now, I have no doubt that she would not have done the same in hindsight, as the education she would have received moving around Africa would have been far more useful than learning about deferred taxation and remuneration trusts! However, you cannot change the past.

Molly had learned many things on her travels, from herbal medicines to witchcraft, from curing animal skins to finding water in the desert. She truly was a remarkable woman, of that there was no doubt. She had also learned that it is how you see yourself that is important, not how others perceive you. This was how she had gained the reputation for being a little eccentric. Thankfully for Zoe, Molly had lived a fairly normal life while she was at school and had worked in an office. This had been a real strain for Molly who pined for the open spaces that she had left behind, but she knew it was the best thing for Zoe. This is something Zoe had never known and Molly had never mentioned. However, all through Zoe's formative years, Molly had kept up her interest in the occult and alternative cultures and lifestyles and as soon as Zoe had secured a place at university, she had sold up and moved to Barnoldswick. She had chosen the area because of its rich heritage, particularly Pendle Hill and the associated history of witchcraft.

For many years she had run her shop, primarily for the benefit of tourists, trying to further people's understanding of what was not considered 'mainstream', as well as acting as a meeting point for like-minded individuals. These tended to be the same people who would congregate around Stonehenge at the summer solstice or were to be found sitting on the protest lines when new runways were being built at airports. This was one reason why Zoe had not had a close relationship with her mother from that point onwards and indeed rarely travelled back to see her during vacation times from college. She tended to stay in or around Manchester which was how she came to end up living and working where she did. She had used the excuse of having found jobs as an intern in various accountancy firms as the reason she didn't come home, but Molly knew what lay beneath the unnecessary excuses. She understood. She always understood. It was a shame that Zoe never got to know the real Molly, but it was too late now.

'Go and talk to your son,' said Zoe impatiently.

It never ceased to amaze Jasper that Dave always became 'his son' when things like this happened. He was 'his son' when the football had come through the lounge window, showering both of them with glass. He was 'his son' when the downstairs toilet had over flowed and three cuddly toys and a cufflink had been unceremoniously recovered from the U-bend. Now was another of those times. Jasper knew there was no sense in arguing, so he smiled as best he could and headed off up the stairs.

Dave's bedroom door was typical for a twelve year old. First of all it was shut and on the outside was a 'Do Not Enter' sign, a skull and crossbones and an anti-nuclear yellow and black sticker. Jasper knocked. There was little chance that he was going to be heard as he could feel the wood panels of the door vibrating to the bass of Dave's CD player which was pumping out something that Jasper didn't recognise. He smiled to himself. How little things change between generations, he thought, remembering how his room had looked almost identical, although the music had been coming from his record player rather than a CD player. He knocked again, a little harder this time, and was greeted by a reluctant 'Come in.'

Dave was lying on his bed looking up at the ceiling. Jasper moved across and sat down next to him. Dave made no attempt to turn the music down. A last act of defiance, thought Jasper, who could remember doing the same thing when his father had come in for a chat. He leant across and turned the music down himself.

'It's not easy for us either, you know.' Jasper started trying the sympathy route. 'Every time we go away on business we have to go through the whole rigmarole of trying to find someone who is prepared to look after you. I know you think it is easy, but it isn't.'

Dave just lay there, not taking his eyes off the same spot on the ceiling he had been looking at ever since his father had come into the room.

'Sure it is,' he said. 'You always farm me out to Uncle Pete, which is fine. He's great. We get on really well, we know each other's likes and dislikes and we just get on with it. But Dad, come on – Grandma?'

'I know it may seem a little harsh,' said Jasper

trying to sound understanding, 'but trust me, it is the only sensible solution. We really can't put upon Bob's family, although I am quite sure they would say yes if we asked them. No, this really has to be family and as Pete is away on one of his round Britain bike trips, I'm afraid Grandma is the only option. I know you are not going to believe this, but she really is an amazing woman if you take the time to get to know her.'

It was becoming quite obvious to Jasper that no matter what he said he was never going to convince Dave of the wisdom of the suggestion. Similarly Dave had resigned himself to the fact that he was going to be spending the next 10 days locked up with a crazy woman, 75 miles away from where his secret life was going to be continuing, but without him!

Chapter 2

Dave's heart sank as he saw his parent's car disappear around the corner of Esp Lane and head off towards the centre of Barlick. Their next stop was home to finish packing and then very early the next morning to Manchester Airport, then a flight to Prague. He was left standing outside his grandmother's terraced house wondering what he had truly done to deserve this.

He had to admit, though, that he had been pleasantly surprised at seeing Grandma again. Because she didn't visit much, it had been a couple of years since he had seen her and she was a lot younger than he had remembered. This should have been no surprise if he had thought about it, because his mother had not been very old when he was born and his grandmother was only 21 years older than his mother. Elspeth was still waving madly, even though all that could be seen of his parent's car was the drifting exhaust smoke.

She turned to look at him. 'Well, just you and me now,' she said, sounding a site more cheerful than Dave felt.

His grandmother was dressed in cheesecloth from head to toe as far as Dave could tell. This was not exactly a style that could be considered current, not even one that could be regarded as 'retro.' Secretly there was a part of Dave that was admiring his grandmother's total lack of regard for what others thought about her. There was the same renegade air about her as there was about Uncle Pete. Suddenly Dave got a mental image of Elspeth sitting on the back of Uncle Pete's bike as he headed down the open road. This made him smile.

'I'm glad you're looking happy,' said Elspeth, completely misreading the situation. 'I was worried that you were going to be devastated being stuck with an old duffer like me.'

Dave didn't have time to respond before she turned and walked back in to her house. It was probably for the best, as he would have scored no points if he had corrected her and she might as well think he was up for it rather than knowing he was there under protest.

His parents hadn't even stopped to come in. They had dropped him off in such a hurry that there hadn't been any time, and if the truth had been known, that was how Zoe had arranged it. She had no wish to travel back in the car smelling of joss sticks, nor did she want to start her journey with a cup of herbal tea, which as far as she could tell had no tea in it, just herbs, and smelled and tasted like medicine.

Dave picked up his bag and dragged it into the house with a heavy heart. In truth, this was the first time he had ever been to his grandmother's house and he had no idea what to expect. Sure, he had a mental picture built up on comments he had heard his parents make about her and spiced up with the infrequent visits she had made to them at Christmas. His most endearing memory was of one year when she and Uncle Pete had started giggling, apparently uncontrollably, on the sofa and Uncle Pete had fallen into the Christmas tree as he tried to get up to go to the bathroom. His mother had been beside herself, his father had left to go to the kitchen to get the vacuum cleaner, or so he thought. In reality he had had to leave the room as he had tears running down his face and didn't want Zoe to see. Dave had been bundled out of the room while they retrieved Uncle Pete from a tangle of fairy lights and all he could remember were the peals of laughter still coming from the sofa. At this he smiled again and hoped his visit wasn't going to be as bad as he first imagined.

'Top of the stairs,' said Elspeth as he closed the front door, 'both sets of stairs. Hope it's OK with you.'

'Thanks,' said Dave as he wondered if he would manage to lug the bag all the way up on his own. The first set of stairs was not too bad. Wide enough that he didn't drag his bag against the wall and not so steep that he thought he was going to fall. The second set was something else altogether! It became obvious fairly quickly that this was a loft conversion and that he was going to be sleeping in the roof. Great, he thought to himself as he heaved his case up the last few steps. He backed into the door, opening it with his elbow and then fell in to the room, literally, as he had managed to get one foot caught on the strap of his bag. He hit the floor with a crash and found himself lying flat on his back looking up at the inside of the roof.

Dave blinked. He could not believe the amazing sight that lay in front of him. It was truly like looking up in to the heavens. The ceiling was made almost entirely of glass and he was, indeed, looking at the stars. The evening was crystal clear, without a cloud in the sky. He was looking straight up at what he thought was the Orion's Belt constellation and he could see every detail. He lay there, not trying to get up, just marvelling at how much light the stars gave off. He then realised that set into the non-glass areas of the ceiling were hundreds of small light bulbs and it was, in fact, them that was giving the room a magical glow. Once the initial excitement of what he had discovered had worn off, he slowly rose to his feet and looked around for a lamp. A beautiful old standard lamp stood by the side of the bed which was tucked into one corner of the room under the sloping roof.

'Be careful you don't bang your head when you get in to bed,' shouted his grandmother from somewhere below him in the house.

'Thanks, Gran,' shouted Dave and he swung his bag up on to the bed so that he could unpack.

The room was simply furnished with a wardrobe and a chest of drawers. It didn't need anything else and to be honest had there been a lot more furniture it would have detracted from the charm of the room and its incredible vista. Dave emptied his case and hung up his favourite outfits. The remainder of his clothes were unceremoniously stuffed in to drawers and he looked around for the TV. Where was it? Surely there must be one here somewhere. What else was he supposed to plug his X-Box into? Slowly the traumatic reality dawned on him. There wasn't one. He had been abandoned in a house where there was no TV in his room. He felt sure that there was some mistake and that once he had had a chat with Gran she would move one up there for him.

He hung his wash kit on the back of the door and thought he would leave it in the bathroom later. It was obvious that it must be on the first floor as there was only one room up in the loft, and no sign of any plumbing there. He was used to his own bathroom, as his parents had an en suite, leaving the family bathroom to him and guests, on the odd occasion that anyone was staying with them. This was going to be interesting having to share with someone, and he made a mental note to try and minimise the impact of his unpleasant innards!

With his unpacking complete, he made his way down the stairs, stopping to notice which door led to the toilet so that he could find it in the night if needed. The other two doors had to be to his grandmother's room and the spare bedroom. He guessed she had put him in the roof to benefit from the amazing view and was glad that she had.

Dave could hear his grandmother busying herself downstairs, probably in the kitchen. He tried to imagine what she would be preparing for supper. From her outward appearance he expected to find bean sprouts, tofu and an array of organic vegetables. Given the choice, he would be sitting down to a nugget meal with a chocolate milkshake, but this seemed somewhat unlikely under the circumstances. He turned and headed down the final set of stairs to the hallway. Gently, he pushed open the door to the lounge and walked in to a veritable Aladdin's cave.

He stood there absolutely motionless as he surveyed the incredible contents of the room. All around him, covering every inch of surface, were more trinkets, knick-knacks and artefacts – he wasn't actually sure what to call them – than he had ever seen in his life. There were little statues, carvings, crystals, wooden ornaments and things that he had no idea of what they were. To be honest, he had no idea what most of them were. There was an old globe which spun on a brass axis and some intricate-looking scientific instruments which looked as though they should be in a museum. The more he looked, the more he discovered. For every piece he could see, there were two or three more behind them, hidden from initial view. There were two chairs; no room for any more. A large plant was growing in one corner. Dave thought it was a rubber plant, but he wasn't really sure. It climbed from a delicate-looking terracotta pot and made its way up the wall and along the join with the ceiling. From there it hung down, giving the impression of standing in a rainforest or perhaps the hot-house in a zoo. The whole place was truly amazing. The walls could hardly be seen because everywhere Dave looked, he saw paintings. The more he looked the more he counted and the more he could see that they had all been painted by the same hand.

There were scenes of storm-tossed seas with sailing boats that looked as if they were about to capsize or be thrown mercilessly against sinister-looking rocks. There were buildings, mostly old buildings, some of which were on fire and others that seemed to be falling down, possibly in the middle of an earthquake. Others were beautiful landscapes of brooding hills with heavy skies. Dave assumed this was probably a local artist and that the hills were those of the local area. He was used to the Peak District and enjoyed getting out to walk across the moors at the weekends with his parents. He had noticed how similar the hills had been as they had approached Barlick in the fading light and was secretly looking forward to getting out and exploring.

Dave turned and stepped back into the hallway. He walked into the next room, which was undoubtedly the dining room, and through into the kitchen where his grandmother was working at the stove.

'Come on in, Dave, and make yourself at home. I know it must be a little disconcerting being dropped off here when you don't really know me from Adam. All I can say is that you may want to forget everything that your mother may have said about me and make up your own mind. I'm not crazy, maybe a little eccentric, but something tells me that we are going to get on just fine. I hope you like nuggets, they happen to be a favourite of mine.'

He could not believe his ears. Perhaps this was going to work out after all.

Dave sat down at the table in the dining room and watched his grandmother slicing potatoes and cutting them into chips. This was actually going to be a rare treat, having chips made from scratch. Normally he was used to eating from McDonalds or having frozen fries heated up in the oven. He had seen his mother making them from scratch perhaps once or twice, but that had been when they had company. Elspeth was now drying the potato slices on a teatowel and Dave was curious as to whether this had a purpose or it was just one of her little idiosyncrasies. She saw him looking somewhat puzzled so she turned to explain.

'It stops the hot fat from reacting with the water on the potatoes when you drop them into the pan,' she said as she checked the heat.

Dave was relieved to find there was a good explanation and that this wasn't the first of many expected signs of craziness. She then dropped a small piece of bread into the pan to see how quickly it went brown. Smiling with obvious contentment she fished out what was now a crouton and started to carefully slide the chips into the oil. While all this was going on, Dave took the opportunity to scan the dining room. It was with no surprise that he once again found a collection of bewildering items, some on the mantlepiece, some behind glass in the corner cabinet and others stacked neatly on a variety of shelves. No matter which way he looked, he found more paintings. This time there was a horse and cart, a long boat making its way through a lock and a group of African warriors which looked strangely out of place among all the others.

'Gran,' he said, as she removed the first batch of chips from the pan, 'where did you get all these paintings?'

Elspeth didn't turn to answer as she was concentrating on not burning herself on the hot oil.

'Oh,' she replied in a slightly distracted manner, 'I didn't get them anywhere. I painted them all. It's a hobby of mine.'

Dave sat there for a moment thinking, and then said, 'Why so many?'

Elspeth laughed.

'I've been painting for a long time, Dave, and each one has a special meaning to me. It would be a shame not to have them out where I can see them.'

Elspeth slid a second pile of chips into the pan and Dave heard the bubbling roar as they hit the piping hot oil. The steam rose from the stove and Elspeth turned to open the fridge, pulling out a large bottle of milk.

'Milkshake OK to go with these?' she asked, holding up a tub of Belgian chocolate ice cream. Dave smiled back. So far things were working out very well.

'Come and grab these, will you?' she said motioning to the knives and forks with her head as she drained the last of the chips and rolled them on a paper towel. 'The ketchup is in the fridge and the salt and vinegar are in the cupboard up to your right.'

Dave did as requested and set the table. As he came back into the kitchen she was just putting the plates on a tray to bring it all through to the dining room. Dave cast an eye over the feast that met entirely with his approval.

'Gran,' he said, not quite sure how to broach the subject, 'is this what you normally eat?'

He was worried that it seemed a little impertinent, but couldn't help himself. He was half wondering if this strange woman was in fact not so strange, and whether he was going to look forward to meal times while staying with her.

'What were you expecting?' asked Elspeth, trying desperately to hide a smile that was creeping across her face, 'Mung beans and lentils?'

Dave felt a little stupid, but one look at her face reassured him that she saw the funny side of it. He followed her through to the table and they sat down to their satisfying meal.

By now, Dave was sure this was going to be an OK experience. He wasn't sure what tomorrow might bring, but nuggets, chips, chocolate milkshakes and a private view of the cosmos from his bed seemed a reasonable start to his first day.

Chapter 3

Dave woke around 6:30 and immediately realised the downside of having a glass ceiling. The sun was streaming into his bedroom and no matter how hard he tried to keep his eyes shut, the glare was too much for him. Grudgingly, he slid out of bed and looked out over the local hills. The previous night, he had not really been able to see the scenery, only marvel at the incredible view that the stars had provided for him. Now he could see the beauty of the moors. He could see why Elspeth had painted them and why she seemed so happy living where she did. Congleton was great as far as Dave was concerned, but it was more the people that he knew and the fact that his friends were there when he needed them that made the town for him. Sure, the Peak District was on the doorstep, but you needed a car to get out to it. Even to get to 'The Cloud' you required a lift or a good three-quarters of an hour on your bike. Here, you just walked out of the back garden and you were on the hillside.

Dave crept down the stairs hoping not to wake Elspeth. He need not have worried. His grand-mother had been up for some time.

'Good morning, Dave,' said Elspeth as she busied herself in the kitchen. 'I assume you are not used to getting up at this time judging by the look on your face,' she said, watching Dave rubbing his eyes.

She was not wrong. Dave was more used to greeting the world at around 10 o'clock when his favourite cartoon show came on. He pulled up a chair and plonked himself down. Elspeth smiled. It had been a long time since she had greeted anyone quite so down in the mouth at breakfast. It was probably when Zoe was about his age.

'Do you drink tea or coffee yet?' asked Elspeth, not quite sure what children drank these days.

'Neither,' replied Dave, wondering if she really would have brewed him some coffee had he said yes. 'Milk will be fine, thanks. Normally I drink squash or diet coke during the day, but always milk at breakfast. Mum always says it will make my bones strong.'

Elspeth smiled. This is what she had always told Zoe growing up and it pleased her to see that she had taken it on board. No matter how hard we try, we always end up a little bit like our parents, she thought to herself. This was a rough translation of one of the 'wisdoms' given to her by a Masai warrior. Most people would hate to admit it, and indeed often people go out of their way to be totally different. However, it is a wise person who realises that generations can pass on thoughts and customs that still have a meaning and it is indeed a sign of respect when these thoughts are gratefully accepted and passed down.

'We can pick up a few things at Leo's in the town later on,' said Elspeth as she poured out a large glass of milk for Dave. 'Cereal to go with that?' She opened a cupboard and pulled out Cheerios, Nesquick and chocolate flakes. Dave had been quite sure that Alpen or All Bran would have been his only choices.

Time passed quickly as they chatted over their meal that finished with toast and marmite. Conversation seemed to flow easily and Dave realised that he had actually enjoyed himself since he had arrived.

'Sorry about all the early morning sunlight,' said Elspeth as she started to clear the dishes. 'It's the price you pay for the amazing view of the night sky. If it bothers you, I have a pair of eye shades that I kept from my last flight to Kenya. Just let me know and you can borrow them if you like.'

Dave passed the dirty dishes through to his grandmother and then he put away the place mats.

Next to the dresser he noticed an easel and paints, along with a painting that that was not yet finished. He bent down to pick it up and held it at arms' length to admire what his grandmother had done so far. It was another moorland scene that seemed to capture the early morning sunlight as it came from low in the sky. It had great depth and colour and seemed to shine with a purple hue from the heather on the hillside.

'Where's this?' he asked, wondering if he was going to get the chance of seeing it in the flesh, as it were.

'Weets Hill,' came the reply. 'It's the big hill directly out the back of the house. I was hoping to get some more done this morning if that's OK with you. I like to get out there early, as the light is fabulous.'

'Just give me time to change,' said Dave, excited at the thought of getting out on to the moors.

'Not so fast, young man,' said Elspeth, a smile playing across her lips. 'I may not be as bad as you thought I was going to be, but I am still a grandmother and we are not going anywhere until you have washed and brushed your teeth.'

Dave groaned. What was it with adults? he thought to himself.

Chapter 4

Elspeth finished packing her painting gear into a shoulder bag and then she dropped in a couple of apples, some crisps and biscuits, bread, cheese, a container of water and a couple of cans of drink. It was likely to be warm this morning and she didn't want Dave getting too thirsty as there were no shops up on the moor. Come to think of it, there wasn't much of anything. A few farm buildings and the odd barn conversion where people now lived. That was the charm of the place. In no time at all you could be out of the town and completely surrounded by nature. She knew that Dave liked the outdoors, so she had no concerns at all about heading up there this morning to get some more of her painting done. All of her paintings felt special to her when she was working on them, but somehow this one seemed extra special. She had managed to capture not only the colours and hues of the hill, but she felt she had captured the feel of it as well, and this pleased her.

'Ready, Gran?' asked Dave as he came barrelling down the stairs.

She smiled. She saw much of herself in him; his enthusiasm for life, his love of the outdoors, the simple way that a 12 year old looked at the world. What a shame, she thought, that children grow up and become so cynical about life. Why couldn't Zoe have kept even a trace of such naïve simplicity?

'Let's make like a horse turd and hit the trail,' said Elspeth.

'Gran!' shouted Dave. 'Mum has a fit if I speak like that.'

'Well,' said Elspeth thoughtfully, 'your Mum is in Prague, so I guess I can say what I like!'

And with that, they left the house and walked down the lane to Town Head. Dave and Elspeth chatted as they made their way up Manchester Road. They turned on to Moorgate and very quickly they left the houses behind them and Dave noticed that the tarmac had given way to the dirt and stones of an unmade road. The hedges hung heavy with leaves weighed down by busy insects making it seem like they were walking through a tunnel. The brilliant flashes of colour supplied by the tall foxgloves broke up the intense green of the privet, and butterflies gently flicked past Dave, looking for shafts of sunlight to warm their wings. Birds darted from hedge to hedge and the low hum of the insects was interrupted by the periodic call of a skylark gently alighting in the grass, or the far-off lilting call of the curlew. Truly this was a magical place. Let's face it, that was why Elspeth had moved here. She had visited a number of times before making the break with her previous life. There was no doubt that it was the right thing to do as she had felt a strange calling from her first visit. Somehow it felt right, almost as if Barlick was trying to tell her that this was where she should be.

The unlikely pair slowly made their way up the steepening trail, while the sun shone down from a cloudless sky. The hedges began to give way to dry stone walls and Dave noticed a house coming closer on the left. Elspeth had a contented look on her face and said very little. She was enjoying the moment as she always did when she walked on Weets Hill.

'If you are thirsty you can sup from the water coming out on the left,' Elspeth declared as they reached Standridge House.

Dave looked up and saw that there was a pipe protruding from the wall a few feet in front of them. Water trickled down into what was probably an old horse trough and then overflowed into the lush green grass below it. Dave looked at the pipe and then at Elspeth.

'Are you serious, Gran? Mum would go mental if she knew I had drunk from something as unhygienic as that.'

Elspeth laughed.

'Your mother has drunk from a lot worse places than that when she was younger,' she said. 'The sad thing is she has forgotten all about it. She has become too caught up in the conveniences of the modern world and takes too much for granted.'

With that she held out her cupped hand and let the refreshingly cold water dance across her palm. With the deft movement of someone who had obviously done this many times before, she raised her hand to her mouth and drank deeply.

'Wonderful,' she said, 'truly wonderful. You must try it.'

With a slightly disbelieving smile Dave moved forward, ready to give it a go. He tried to copy what Elspeth had done, but somehow the water just ran through his fingers and by the time his hand got to his mouth, there was nothing left to drink. Again he tried; same result. Finally, with a degree of frustration, he cupped one hand under the other and successfully brought the clear liquid to his lips. She was right, it did taste wonderful. It had an earthy quality which was different to the chlorinated, fluorinated water he was used to drinking from the tap at home. He took a second draught and then splashed what was left across his face.

'Ready?' asked Elspeth.

'Absolutely,' replied Dave and they continued up the hill.

Not long past the farm, Elspeth moved over to the right of the path and pointed to a stile.

'Here is where we leave the road,' she said, 'and where we get the earth beneath our feet.'

Dave looked up and saw a small wooden signpost with a dark brown witch burned, or perhaps carved, into it.

'Part of the Pendle Witch Trail,' explained Elspeth when she saw him looking at the sign. 'You will find those all around Barlick and beyond. There are miles of beautiful walks circling these hills. Amazing views, too, out towards the Ribble Valley and over the tops toward Blacko. We'll be able to see a wind farm from the summit.'

Dave had no idea what a wind farm was, but the thought of what it might be began playing in his mind. Rather than ask, he came up with visions of trees laden with clouds ripe for the picking, bushes strewn with wisps of breezes waiting to be plucked by passers-by, perhaps to be released later on a still day to help dry the washing. It was clear that Dave was in his element. What had begun as a trip he was dreading was turning out all right after all.

Elspeth climbed through the narrow gap in the wall and down on to the grass beyond. A sheep, who had been minding its own business, suddenly realised it was no longer alone and scurried across the field, starting a chain reaction with the other sheep nearby. Dave followed her through, marvelling at the skill of the workmen that had built the miles of wall that he could see – and all without the use of cement.

'A farthing a yard, was what they used to pay for these walls and you were expected to find your own stone.' Elspeth spoke in the tone that older people use when they are trying to remind you how hard it was when they were your age.

Dave looked at her with a quizzical expression.

'What's a farthing?' he asked having never heard of such a thing.

Elspeth laughed. 'I guess you've never come across one of those. Way too young. I doubt even your parents remember them. Back before we changed to today's decimal currency, we had a rather more complicated system here in this country. We still had pounds, but they were broken down into 20 shillings. Each shilling had 12 pennies, making 240 pennies to the pound, not the 100 we have today. Each penny was broken down into two halfpennies and each halfpenny was broken down into two farthings, so each farthing was a quarter of a penny. So, there were 960 farthings to a pound and they paid people one of those for every yard, near enough a metre, of wall that they built.'

Dave looked at her in astonishment. He didn't even bother to bend down and pick up change in the street unless it was silver in colour, and a 5p piece was equivalent to 48 yards of wall! 'Unbelievable,' he thought to himself. He was sure Elspeth wouldn't be lying to him, but how could anyone get paid so little for doing so much hard work? How could anyone have lived with such a complicated system of money, either?

With that question playing on his mind, he followed Elspeth along what was now little more than a slightly worn path in the grass. The hill gave way to his right and down into a wide valley. He could see farm buildings way off in the distance through a gentle heat haze that made everything shimmer in the sunlight. Ahead of them he could see the wall trailing up the left side of the field, but could not see how far it went because his view was interrupted by another wall cutting across the top of the pasture. He didn't know how far away the top of Weets would be, but truthfully it didn't matter.

Suddenly the ground to his left dropped away into what looked like a pudding basin.

'What's this?' he asked pointing at the huge depression in the ground.

'A sink, or swallow hole,' came the reply.

Dave was getting more and more impressed with Grandma as time passed.

'This is one cool lady,' he thought to himself. 'How can my mother possibly be related to her?'

Elspeth stopped to catch her breath and to admire the greens and greys of the landscape that were punctuated by the off-white of the sheep and the blue sky interrupted by the fluffy clouds that were slowly being burned off by the sun.

A strange shriek broke the silence and brought her thoughts back to the here and now.

'Just a grouse,' said Elspeth, without

even thinking.

Dave was amazed. She seemed to be able to answer his questions before he even got a chance to ask them. Was there something magical about his grandmother? he wondered.

The truth was that Elspeth automatically explained things to 'off-comed-uns.' This was a local expression for anyone not originally from Barlick. Elspeth also fell in to this category, but compared with Dave she was a local; nothing more mysterious than that.

Dave ran over to get a better look at the hole. It is something genetic in boys, the absolute need to explore strange things, to climb on walls and to keep cool bugs in glass jars. Dave dived down the steep sides and looked back up at Elspeth with a grin.

'You find them all over the north of England. It is nothing more dramatic than the ground collapsing into a gap left by a mine, a fault, or more often than not, a gap created by an underground stream over many centuries. There are loads of them in Derbyshire because the rocks are mainly limestone which is more easily eroded by running water. That's why people chose to build their houses out of granite or gritstone when they could, so that they weathered better and wouldn't get literally washed away.'

Dave was amazed. His grandmother knew no end of things and just dropped them matter-of-factly into conversations rather than trying to show how clever she was. He rummaged around, trying to see if he could find 'a hole at the bottom of the hole' that would let him see into the bowels of the earth; sadly not. The grass grew across the floor of the sunken domain in the same way as it did down its sides and over its edges and the ground seemed just as firm as anywhere else as he jumped up and down, hoping to see some magical movement, culminating in the soil opening up and presumably swallowing him. Boys rarely think through the consequences of actions when in 'explorer mode.'

Elspeth had by now disappeared from view and been replaced by a curious sheep who was wondering what this strange creature was doing in its hideaway. Dave moved slowly up the side to try and touch this new friend. No chance. Sheep have to be the most timid creatures ever, in open countryside. As soon as he moved, the sheep turned and bolted. Undaunted, Dave scaled the remaining slope and emerged victorious. He had fulfilled his need to investigate and come through with flying colours. Time to move on.

Elspeth waved to the occupants of the

farmhouse opposite and made her way up the track parallel to the road, until she reached the next dry stone wall where she waited for Dave to catch up. He had the energy inherent in his youthfulness and came bounding up the field behind her. Whether he wanted to admit it to himself or not, he was really enjoying his visit, really enjoying his grandmother's company and really enjoying being out in the fresh air. To one side he had an amazing view over the lower hills towards Skipton and to his other an expanse of moorland, reaching up towards the sky. He could not wait to see what the track beyond this wall would bring.

As soon as they had traversed the stile, the track changed from being worn grassland to being quite rutted and stony. It had obviously been worn away by generations of sheep, walkers and – more recently – mountain bikers, leaving their impressions on the landscape. He remembered a quote from somewhere that said: 'Take only memories, leave only footprints,' and he now felt he knew what they meant. It was a shame that erosion was taking its toll, but reassuring that there was enough 'traffic' to cause it. Such scenery needed to be appreciated and the only way it could be appreciated was to get out of the car and make the effort. Obviously the people of Barlick made the effort to enjoy their surroundings. This was comforting to Dave.

As the two travellers made their way up the hill, the vegetation became more coarse, as grass gave way to heather and bracken. The hillside sloped away ever more steeply to the right and the path became rockier. As they followed the wall around its tortuous twists and turns, the ground suddenly dropped in dramatic fashion where the underlying strata had given way and slipped down the hillside. At the bottom of the slide was a small stream, cutting its way through the mass of rubble, undeterred by the obvious enormity of what had happened probably hundreds of years earlier. Dave's immediate need was to investigate.

'Be very careful,' said Elspeth, who seemed to be aware of the primordial urges for exploration welling up in the boy.

Dave stopped and looked over the steep slopping sides of the slippage.

'The ground will give way again if you tread on it and you will find yourself sliding all the way down, whether you want to or not,' she said. 'You could end up with some nasty cuts and bruises.'

Dave thought it over for a minute. Seemed a reasonable price to pay for what could be great fun, but then he remembered, leave only footprints.

He stepped back, smiled at his grandmother and made his way back to the track.

In his short time there he had learned to respect Weets Hill and did not want to feel that he had inadvertently left any unnecessary destruction. There would be plenty more adventures ahead of him today.

A few deft jumps from rock to rock and Dave was able to traverse the stream as it crossed the path without getting his feet wet. To be honest, there was no need to do anything so athletic and indeed Elspeth just quietly walked through the water, which didn't even come over the soles of her shoes. That wasn't the point though. It was a river that needed to be forded without being swept away to your death!

A final wall, another stile and they would be out on to the top off the hill. Dave climbed the three steps and surveyed the horizon like a pirate looking out from the bridge of his ship. He could see a cairn in the distance. Cairns are piles of rocks that walkers pile up at strategic high points along a path so that others can easily see where they are going. This is particularly useful when fog comes down on the mountains, so that travellers don't mistakenly veer off the track and lose their footing. Elspeth had told him that there was a 'Trig Point' on top of Weets but so far he hadn't seen it. That meant there was still a little way to go. Trig points – triangulation points, to give them their full name – are small white obelisks that are built on the highest points of land. On top of these plinths are three brass indentations or grooves emanating from a central point. If you look down the line of any one of the three, you will see the next trig point in the distance. You can, therefore, triangulate your position, hence the name. Dave knew of them from the Peak District close to where he lived. The three indentations were there so that a theodolite could be placed easily on top of the plinth and really accurate measurements taken.

Knowing that he was not yet at the top spurred him onwards and he leapt down from his 'bridge', ready to board the rival ship.

'Hey! Watch who you're treading on, matey!'

Chapter 5

Dave nearly fell over in surprise. He had almost landed on a boy who looked to be about his own age, who was kneeling at the bottom of the wall.

'Wicked bug just crawled in here,' he said, trying desperately to wiggle a finger into a hole that was obviously far too small.

Dave crouched down to see if he could help, or at least see what it was that the boy was chasing. Boys have no need for introductions and certainly need not exchange names before immediately bonding around something important like insects.

'Went in here somewhere,' said the boy, trying to move boulders held in place by the weight of the entire wall and not surprisingly making no headway.

'Can I help?' asked Dave, immediately getting in to the thrill of the chase.

'Nah,' came the reply. 'It'll be long gone by now.'

Both boys stood up and for the first time they got a good look at each other. Dave was reasonably tall for his age, but this boy was taller than him. Whereas Dave was quite well-built, this lad was almost painfully thin. His hair was black and was being ruffled by the gentle breeze that caressed the moor. His face could certainly be described as kind looking and there was a cheeky grin that seemed to reach almost from ear to ear.

Dave smiled back, not really knowing what to say.

Just at that moment Elspeth came panting over the wall.

'Hi,' she said, as if it was the most natural thing in the world. 'And who might you be?'

'Jen,' he said, 'short for Jensen,' and he held his hand out towards Elspeth.

'Nice to meet you, Jen,' she said firmly shaking him by the hand. 'I'm Elspeth and this is my grandson Dave. He's twelve, how old are you?'

Amazing, thought Dave, she just cleared up all the immediate mysteries by asking a couple of questions. Why did such initial pleasantries always seem so impossible to him?

'I'm thirteen,' said Jen and turning toward Dave, once again stuck his hand out. 'Pleasure to meet you, Dave,' he said and genuinely looked like he meant it.

Dave shook his hand, beaming broadly at the thought of having met a potential friend. Gran was great, but this was a kindred spirit, another explorer with whom to partner on the final assault to the top of Weets.

'You new around here?' asked Jen as Elspeth began to head off along the path. 'I don't think I've seen you before and I know most people who come up here.'

'Just visiting for the week,' replied Dave. 'Staying with my Grandma in Barnoldswick.'

'Barlick,' retorted Jen. 'No one who lives around here calls it Barnoldswick.'

'We're heading to the top of Weets,' said Dave as if he felt he needed to explain his presence. 'Fancy tagging along?'

'Sure,' said his new friend, 'but it's not very far; just up beyond that cairn.'

The three travellers slowly made their way across slightly softer ground now. It had a springy give to it and felt like the peat of the Peak District. Here and there were small tufts of cotton grass which Dave and Jen bent down to look at and feel, rolling the soft tips between their fingers.

Elspeth smiled. Rarely had she had a day as good as this in recent memory. She was relishing the time she had been given with Dave and loving the way that he had obviously taken to so many of the things that she dearly loved. Some people would have been jealous of the intrusion of Jen, but Elspeth just absorbed it all as part of a great day, sharing Dave's obvious enjoyment of having found a friend to enjoy the experience with.

They passed by the cairn and Elspeth suggested that the two boys find a couple of stones each to continue the age-honoured tradition of adding to the pile. It quickly became a competition with Dave trying to find the biggest stone possible while Jen went for quantity rather than quality. Elspeth stood amused by the whole comedy being played out before her. The boys were running around like ants desperately bringing back trophies to their hill to impress the queen. Eventually an unspoken truce was agreed between the two and the last couple of stones were balanced precariously on top of the pyramid. Both sweating profusely from their endeavours, the boys started to laugh loudly. It was a sound drawn from pure exhilaration and pleasure. No pretence, nothing withheld, just enjoyment of the moment. Elspeth smiled.

The trig point was now in their sights and as if a gun had just been fired, the boys went racing off towards the top. By the time Elspeth caught up with them, they were sitting on a bench looking out towards the Ribble Valley. The air was clear, the view spectacular and the three of them took a moment to savour the view.

'Drink, anyone?' said Elspeth holding out her water bottle.

Thirsts were quenched with each taking care not to take too much, Dave because he knew there could be a long day ahead of him and Jen, because he was a guest.

'I'm going to set up shop here for a while,' said Elspeth as she unloaded her painting gear. 'Why don't you guys find something to amuse yourselves with, but just don't go so far that I can't see you.'

With that, she started to set up her easel and brought brush after brush out of her shoulder bag. Obviously she had done this many times before because the boys watched transfixed as more things than could possibly have been in the bag came out of it, one after another in a never ending stream.

'Bravo!' shouted Jen and he applauded wildly; Dave quickly joined in.

'I've never seen anything quite so impressive. The Amazing Elspeth and her lovely assistant Dave,' and he bowed with a flourish of his arms. Dave suddenly realised what he had called him and punched him on the shoulder, in a good-hearted way, you understand. Jen laughed and motioned to Dave that they should be going, and the two of them turned to decide in which direction their future lay.

'Be back soon, Gran,' shouted Dave over his shoulder as he and Jen decided that the only possible way to head, for two ardent explorers, was over the edge of the steep hill that stood before them.

Elspeth watched them go and thought that this was not quite what she had meant when she had said stay in sight. 10 seconds into the deal and they had already disappeared from view. Still, she smiled to herself as she clipped a pallet of paints to the side of the easel. Dave was really happy and there was no real harm he could come to on top of Weets Hill.

Over the next couple of hours, Elspeth painted away merrily and Dave and his new best friend Jen appeared at regular intervals from a different direction each time. She would be alerted to their frequent returns by shrieks of laughter followed by the tops of two heads usually at the same time and more often than not in some kind of wrestling hold. Each time they came tumbling on to the scene, Elspeth marvelled at how dirty they had become compared with the previous time. Boys can get filthy just sitting watching television. I bet if you are reading this and you are a boy, if you look at your fingernails now, there will be dirt under at least one of them, so you can imagine the state of the two of them on the moor! They were having a great time.

This time they noticed that Elspeth had laid out some food on a small cloth she had spread on to the bench. The three of them ate heartily, some obviously more than others and Jen thanked Elspeth profusely for being allowed to join in.

'Saved me having to run all the way home,' he said, wiping away some crumbs from the side of his mouth.

'Won't your parents be worried?' asked Elspeth, thinking how concerned she would have been if Dave had been up here on his own all this time and hadn't returned for lunch.

'No problem,' said Jen in a matter-of-fact manner. 'I spend most of my days up here in the holidays and they never know when I am going to turn up. They are very laid back about it. I know every inch of the moor and tend to lose track of time.'

The boys were obviously eager to get going again and immediately leapt to their feet as soon as the last biscuit had been swallowed.

'Can I see what you are painting?' asked Jen just before he was felled by a flying rugby tackle from Dave.

'Of course,' replied Elspeth, 'but it isn't nearly finished yet.'

Jen and Dave came around to the front of the canvas and both were obviously impressed with what she had produced so far. In front of them was a watercolour that captured the subtle hues of the moorland and the gentle haze of the sky. The painting had a wonderful depth and the boys felt almost as if they could walk into the scene as easily as walking into the real landscape.

'That's brilliant,' said Jen with obvious feeling.

'Gran is a great artist,' said Dave proudly. 'She has a load of other paintings that she has done back at the house. Maybe you could come over and see them later?'

'I'd like that,' said Jen, feeling that he had found a friend. 'What are those?'

Jen was pointing in to the picture. Dave moved closer to see what he was looking at. There were two smudges of darker paint in the middle ground.

'Those,' said Elspeth with a smile, 'are you and Dave.'

The boys smiled.

'They may not look like much at the moment,' she said, 'but by the time I am finished they will definitely be you. I have always included people in my paintings ever since I lived in Africa. The people I stayed with believed that if you could capture the likeness of a person, then you could keep them alive for ever. Their spirit would endure through the canvas.'

'Wow!' said Jen 'You are one cool lady.'

Elspeth smiled. Dave smiled even more. 'Yeh,' he thought to himself, 'she is one cool lady, my grandmother.'

Then the boys were off again.

The afternoon rolled slowly on under the ever-increasing glare of the sun. The morning clouds had been burned away until there was virtually an uninterrupted blue sky as far as the eye could see. There was an unmistakeable increase in the activity of the insect population as dragonflies, beetles and various bees and wasps went about their daily business. Every now and then one would land on Elspeth's canvass as if alighting on a tuft of heather, stay a while and then move on to more fertile ground. Elspeth carried on painting with the quiet assured strokes of an artist who had repeated this scene a million times. A little more green here, a little more brown there, and slowly the picture came to life.

In the background she could hear the shrieks of the two boys as they wrestled, repelled pirate ships and generally saved the world from a variety of evil-doers.

Elspeth noticed that the shadows being cast by her easel were getting longer and she looked at her watch. Four o'clock. She turned and waved to Dave and he and Jen came running over to see what she wanted.

'Sorry, boys,' she said, 'but I am going to have to break this party up. Dave and I need to be heading home.'

Not surprisingly Dave and Jen both let out a sigh and tried to argue for an extra 30 minutes.

'If Jen wants to, and he clears it with his parents, he can come round later this evening and the two of you can play for a while. How does that sound?'

'Sounds good to me,' said Jen, smiling at Dave.

'Me too. Thanks, Gran.'

With that settled, Elspeth put away her paints and tipped out the dirty water she had been using to mix her colours. Not wanting to miss a moment, the boys took the opportunity to put each other into head locks.

The three figures then made their way back to the stile where Dave had started his new friendship by almost landing on top of Jen.

'I'll say goodbye here,' said Jen as Dave and Elspeth made their way over the wall. 'My dad won't be home from work for a while and mum is going to Asda in Colne, so I might as well stay out and enjoy the rest of the afternoon. How does 7:30 sound round at your place?'

'Perfect,' said Elspeth and she gave Jen the address. 'We will see you later then.' She turned to head back down to Barlick with Dave scurrying from side to side like a sheepdog trying to herd a flock down the hillside.

Chapter 6

'It's only 7:40,' said Elspeth trying to calm Dave down. 'He's only 10 minutes late.'

Dave was bouncing off the walls. It may only have been 10 minutes to his grandmother, but it seemed like an age to him.

Since getting back from their afternoon on Weets, Dave had been watching every single minute click past on the lounge clock. He had been trying to watch television, but with every rotation of the hands he knew that he was one minute closer to getting back outside to play. Time had never moved so slowly. He had even wolfed down his tea, thinking that once that was out of the way, Jen was bound to turn up. Elspeth was horrified to see her hard work vacuumed down without apparently touching the sides and was quite sure Dave was going to be awake all night suffering with indigestion. Little did she know the constitution of a boy on a mission!

7:45.

'Where is he?' asked Dave almost bursting at the seams.

By now he was looking out of the front window, willing Jen to appear from down the street.

'Just sit quietly,' pleaded Elspeth, 'you're driving me insane. Although most people around here think I'm pretty much there already.'

Dave smiled. Her sense of humour had helped, just a little, to keep things in perspective.

'You're not mad, Gran,' he said reassuringly, 'just a little eccentric.'

He chose his words precisely to mimic those of his mother when referring to Elspeth. Elspeth knew this and smiled back, amused by his quick wit.

At 8:00 the two of them snuggled down to watch one of Dave's favourite programmes and while this didn't make him forget the late arrival of his new friend, it certainly distracted him for half an hour. Quietly Elspeth looked at the clock and wondered what was keeping Jen. They had no way of contacting him as they didn't even know his surname. They assumed he lived in Barlick as he was on foot, but he could have lived in one of the nearby towns as well. She knew how disappointed Dave was going to be if he didn't show.

'Perhaps his parents already had something planned for tonight,' said Elspeth, hoping that that was the case and that Dave would understand. 'He doesn't know how to contact us to let us know if he can't make it.'

'I know,' he groaned. 'Why didn't we think to exchange phone numbers?'

'Too late now,' came the reply, which while accurate, was not really what he wanted to hear. 'Best just work on the basis that we won't see him tonight, but we will be able to find him tomorrow. We can always walk back up Weets if he doesn't show early on.'

Dave knew she was right and had to accept that it was to be an evening of Gran and the television. Sensing his disappointment, she went into the kitchen, coming back moments later with two thick chocolate milkshakes; always a good second best in such circumstances.

After drinking his shake, Dave asked if he could see Elspeth's painting from earlier. She was glad that he was interested in what she had done and went out to the hall to collect her work. It was wrapped in a piece of muslin which she lovingly removed to ensure that the painting was not damaged. She laid the canvas on the cushion of an easy chair so that the light from the lamp hit it like a spotlight. Dave studied every square inch as though he were an art critic for a major newspaper.

'You know, Gran, that really is very good.' Elspeth beamed. 'I don't know why, but those two figures couldn't be anyone else but Jen and me. Is it OK if I show him the finished article tomorrow?'

'Of course. I just hope he likes it as much as you do.'

The rest of the evening passed uneventfully and relatively quietly, save for the intermittent laughter that accompanied 'Never Mind The Buzzcocks.' Dave was well impressed that his Gran was going to let him watch it and was then even more impressed when she said it was one of her favourites!

'A little irreverent,' she explained, 'which is probably why I like it so much.' That in itself made Dave chuckle.

Soon after it finished, he made his excuses and headed off to bed. Partly because he thought that the sooner he went off to sleep, the sooner the morning would be there and partly so that he could lie there and look up at the stars as the evening sky had stayed as clear as the afternoon had been.

'Can you take the painting up with you?' asked Elspeth as he headed out of the lounge. 'They tend to dry better up in the top room.'

Dave grabbed it, being careful not to touch the front of the canvas, and studiously steered it up the two flights of stairs to his room. He propped it up in one corner and then made himself ready for bed.

Looking up through the attic window, he could not only make out Orion, but particularly Orion's belt. He always thought of the movie *Men in Black* whenever he saw this constellation. He was fairly sure he could make out Cassiopeia ... and wasn't that Aurega?

That was the last thing he remembered until he awoke with a start. He thought he heard a noise in his room. It is always difficult getting used to the noises of someone else's house; the creaking caused by the central heating going off and the floor-boards adjusting to the change in temperature. The groaning of the roof beams as the cold night air cools the slates and seemingly shifts the whole ceiling. All the little changes that Elspeth was used to by now and slept quietly through. Nothing to worry about, he thought, just unfamiliar sounds of the night. With that, he turned over and started to drop back off to sleep.

There it was again! It took him a moment to realise why it was that it unnerved him so much. It sounded like someone was saying his name. How could that be? He had to be mistaken. He lay there trying not to breathe so that he could listen for the noise again. Nothing. He sat up, hoping to catch the sound of his name and see where it was coming from. Perhaps his grandmother was calling him from downstairs. He looked at his watch, pressing the button that made the face light up. 02:45. Way too late for her calling, unless she had had an accident and needed him. He quickly leapt out of bed and made his way downstairs, being careful not to trip and add to the problem. He stopped outside his Gran's door and listened. All he could hear was the sound of her breathing heavily while she slept. He quietly pushed the door open and looked in on her. She appeared to be sleeping quite peacefully. He gently pulled the door closed, being careful not to wake her, and slowly made his way back upstairs.

'Obviously just a bad dream,' he thought to himself. Perhaps Gran had been right about the indigestion. He smiled at that thought and then lay back down. Within moments he was sound asleep.

Morning came in a blaze of glory, literally. Dave

was suddenly aware that his room had been lit up like a Christmas tree. The sun had already risen high enough in the sky to beam directly into his room, illuminating the whole of the wall above his bed. It was truly a spectacular sight. It was so bright that even through closed eyes Dave could not help but be amazed by the intensity. He leapt out of bed, pulled on his jeans and hoodie and raced downstairs.

'Morning Gran,' he shouted as he sprinted in to the kitchen and greeted her with a hug. Then he stopped. Amazing. He would never have thought to greet his mother in that way, but it seemed so natural to do it this morning. Elspeth picked up on his dilemma and quickly broke the hold of the moment by asking if he wanted cereal or something cooked. Being fairly sure that the 'something cooked' probably involved black pudding, he decided to go for the cereal. As it was, Elspeth was only thinking about bacon and eggs, but he wasn't to know that and his friends in Congleton had convinced him that the people 'up north' pretty much lived on black pudding. Ah well, another day perhaps.

The two of them chatted over breakfast and tried to make plans that included finding Jen. Elspeth knew that Dave's heart was set on getting back together with him and as she had no plans anyway, it didn't bother her about building that day around him.

By 10:00 Jen was a no-show, so they decided to head back up Weets as they had the day before and see if they could happen across him again.

The walk was glorious. The colours seemed more intense, the birdsong sweeter and louder and already the beating sun had warmed the ground itself. Dave raced around, now more familiar with the terrain after one whole day, and he retraced his steps pretty much as he had the day before. The sink hole was quickly navigated, just to ensure that no opening to the underworld had appeared overnight. No such luck. Then it was onward and upward, hoping to find his friend. Elspeth was having trouble keeping up, although she was moving faster today as she had neither lunch nor easel this time. She reckoned that they would either find Jen and then the boys would head back to her house, or they would not find him and they would be back for lunch anyway.

As it was, it was sadly the latter. There was no sign of Jen and despite Dave's valiant attempts to find him, no luck.

Dave slumped into 'his' easy chair in the lounge and switched on the TV. He felt cheated. No sooner had he made a friend than he seemed to have lost him. He turned the satellite to MTV and tried to console himself by watching Britney Spears wearing not much at all. Pleasant on the eye, he thought, but not the same as having a mate to mess around with.

Gran walked in and without explanation said, 'Come on, Dave, we need to head into town.'

It was not until they were already in front of the estate agents near the Cross Keys pub that Elspeth spoke again.

'While I was in the kitchen getting lunch,' she began, 'I was listening to the local radio station. The news finished with an item talking about concern growing for a local boy who failed to return home last night. I'm sure it is not Jen, but I just thought we should go down to the police station and make certain.'

Dave wasn't sure how to react. She must be wrong. It couldn't be Jen. However, he hadn't shown last night when he said he would. Probably just had something to do. Maybe not. Maybe something had happened. All these thoughts were racing through his mind, but he said nothing.

'You OK, Dave?'

He nodded.

'Not far now,' said Elspeth as they cornered the

town square and headed up past the library.

At the traffic lights on Rainhall Road, the two of them entered the police station, both feeling a little apprehensive. Neither had ever been inside such a building before, but Elspeth knew she had to make Dave feel comfortable so she immediately took charge and acted as if this was a regular occurrence for her.

'Just wait here,' she said. 'I'll go and check at the window,' and with that she pressed the bell ring on the counter top to get someone's attention.

Elspeth turned and smiled reassuringly at Dave, trying to put him at ease. Almost immediately a policewoman came out and engaged Elspeth in conversation. After what seemed like only a minute – it couldn't have been much longer – Elspeth came over to Dave and said, 'She asked if we could wait here for a moment.'

They both looked at each other, not knowing quite what to make of it. However, before either could speak, a very earnest-looking, slightly portly man appeared and invited them to join him in an interview room off to one side.

'I'm sure there is nothing to worry about, but we have to be certain.' The man sat heavily in a chair. 'I'm Inspector Wilcox, Brian Wilcox. And you would be?' He raised a pencil to start making notes.

'At what time did you say you left the boy yesterday?' he asked looking at his watch as if this was going to make it easier to remember.

'Soon after four,' replied Elspeth. 'Do you think it might be the same boy?'

'Hard to tell,' said Inspector Wilcox and then he sheepishly looked at Elspeth. 'Probably should have asked you this earlier,' he said, 'but did the boy tell you his name?'

'Jen,' Dave said without hesitation, 'short for Jensen.'

'Thanks,' said the policeman, 'you have both been most helpful. Do you have a number where I can reach you if needed?'

They walked home in silence. Inspector Wilcox hadn't really told them anything. He had asked lots of questions and listened to the answers, taken loads of notes, but had never said if it was Jen they were looking for.

'Why wouldn't he tell us anything?' asked Dave as Elspeth opened the front door.

'Well, until they are ready to release information to the public,' she said slowly, 'the police never confirm or deny anything. They have to take all the facts on board and then they can deal with them accordingly. They don't want to upset the family involved in case there is a good reason for the absence, and they don't want friends worrying when there is nothing they can do.'

Dave looked unconvinced. If it was Jen, he wanted to be out there helping. He had only known him less than a day, but that was all it took. They were fast friends now and he wanted to help.

As soon as they had taken off their shoes, Elspeth put on both the TV and the radio, hoping to pick up on some local news updates. Dave went straight up to his room and lay on his bed looking up at the window. Could it have been Jen? What could he do to find out? What could he do to help? Obviously his grandmother knew the moors pretty well, so they could at least go back and start looking where they had left him the day before.

'Dave.'

There it was again. The same sound he had heard last night. He sat up and looked around. This time he was not dreaming.

'Dave, help me.'

Dave's blood ran cold. There was no mistaking it this time. It was definitely someone calling his name. It seemed far off and eerily detached. He looked around to see if he could pinpoint where it was coming from. He waited patiently to see if the voice came back. Nothing. Time seemed to stand still as he sat motionless on the edge of his bed.

'Dave, over here.'

There it was again. It was definitely coming from within his room and from somewhere in the corner by his door. Dave knew he needed to get up to go over and investigate, yet somehow his arms and legs refused to move. He was frozen to the spot. Fear had gripped him in a way that he had never experienced before. This was definitely the weirdest thing that had ever happened to him. Gradually he managed to gain control of his body again. He inched forward and dropped to his hands and knees. He shuffled across the bedroom floor on all fours, cocking his head to one side in case the voice returned. When he reached the corner he began to move things to one side to see if there was any sign of where the sound was coming from. He didn't know what he was looking for, but it just seemed like the right thing to do. Shoes, comic books, his holdall; all were picked up and gently placed behind him. Dirty socks, Elspeth's painting and a small shoe box that belonged to Elspeth quickly followed.

'Hello,' said Dave, feeling somewhat self-conscious. 'Can you hear me?'

'I'm here,' came a distant reply.

The hairs on the back of Dave's neck stood up.

The voice was closer, but now seemed to be behind him. Slowly he turned his head, almost afraid of what he might see. There was nothing there. Dave's mind began to spin. 'What on earth's happening?' he wondered to himself. 'Am I going mad?'

'Come closer,' said the voice, 'I can't see you any more.'

Dave followed the sounds in an attempt to find its source. It was coming from the pile of things he had moved. 'The shoe box,' he whispered to himself. 'It has to be the shoe box.' He knew that Elspeth had all sorts of mystical things in the house and obviously this was one of them. He slowly picked up his clothes that were laying on top of the pile and moved the painting to one side.

'That's better,' came the voice. 'At least I can see you again.'

Dave moved gingerly towards the shoe box. Mustering all his nerve he picked it up and began to open the lid. He was acting as if he was removing the detonator from a bomb, knowing that one false move could set the whole thing off.

'What are you doing?'

Dave nearly jumped out of his skin. The box lid went one way, the box went the other and the contents spilled out all over the floor. Tubes of paint. His heart was beating like a sparrow's and he could hardly catch his breath.

'I'm over here, look at the painting.'

Chapter 7

Elspeth was pottering around the kitchen, not really being able to settle on anything in particular. She had begun to prepare a meal and then half way through she had started to clean out a cupboard. In her mind she was asking herself the same questions that Dave had been asking himself earlier. She was praying that it wasn't Jen and feeling guilty that even if it wasn't, there was still a missing child from what the news had said.

How would she be feeling if it was Dave that was missing? The thought was almost too unbearable to consider. What would she say to her daughter? How would she ever forgive herself? She, like Dave, came to the conclusion that she had to do something. Anything.

She decided to go up to Dave's room and talk things through with him. Her plan was to head back up on to Weets to where they had left Jen the day before and see if they could pick up on any clues. Even if it wasn't Jen that was missing, she felt she needed to be busy.

Just as she reached the top of the second set of stairs, she stopped. She could hear Dave talking to someone, but knew there was no one else in the house. She stepped forward to try to hear what was being said, but she couldn't pick up on anything through the door, which was firmly shut. She knocked gently, standing back and waiting for the door to be opened. Dave was looking pale as his face slowly appeared in the crack between the door and the frame.

'Gran,' he said faintly, 'I think you had better see this.'

Elspeth stepped into the room and looked around to see who Dave had been talking to. She saw no one but knew she should not question him at this moment. It was obvious he had something important to tell her and he needed to do that in his own time. One of Elspeth's great gifts was knowing when to be silent; something that most of us could learn from.

She sat on the edge of the bed and waited for

Dave to speak. In that moment of silence, she scanned the room and noticed nothing unusual except for the fact that there was a pile of seemingly random articles piled in a heap in the middle of the floor. Clothes, a bag, her painting, a shoe box and some comic books. What had he been looking for and more importantly, what had he found?

'Hi, Elspeth.'

Elspeth turned around to look at Dave. She was a little surprised as this was the first time he had ever used her first name, but she thought she would let it pass under the circumstances.

'Down here.'

Elspeth didn't understand. She was looking at Dave and he had said nothing.

'Down here, on the floor. It's me ... Jen.'

Elspeth's jaw dropped. She couldn't believe her eyes. She was looking at her painting from yesterday and in the foreground was one of the figures, apparently talking to her. Dave was just looking at her. Elspeth quickly realised that this was one of those occasions when she needed to take control and look as if this was one of the most natural things in the world to help Dave deal with it.

'Hello, Jen,' she said, trying not to let the

quiver in her voice come across too badly. 'This is pretty weird,' said Jen.

'You can say that again!' came Dave's reply. 'What's happening, Gran?'

'Why don't we let Jen speak,' she said, not really knowing what else to say.

With that, she and Dave moved closer to the picture, both lying on the carpet as if they were getting comfortable before watching a TV show. Jen was moving around nervously in the painting. Elspeth was transfixed. Was this really what she had painted the day before? Jen looked so real, but he was obviously painted. As he walked from side to side, the grass and heather caught around his feet. As she stared, a bird flew in from left to right across the sky and in the background the sheep appeared to be slowly grazing. This was truly amazing. For some reason she remembered a Robin Williams film where he entered a painting, searching for his wife: *What Dreams May Come*. What a time to remember trivia. But this was real, not a Hollywood movie. Jen was really here, in a painting and talking to them.

'I'm not really sure how I got here,' said Jen, 'but let me tell you what happened after I left you. I knew I had a couple of hours to kill, so I headed off across the hill as I've done a hundred times before. I heard a grouse and decided to see if I could creep up on it. I couldn't see where it was exactly, but I knew it was somewhere ahead of me in the heather, so I dropped on to my hands and knees and slowly crept forward. Then, without warning, the ground seemed to open up under me and I fell. The next thing I remember is waking up lying on my side with an amazing headache. I had landed on a rock and must have knocked myself out. There was blood on my face, but dried blood, so I must have been lying there for some time. When I got up, I was in some kind of a cave. There was a stream running along the floor, but I couldn't see it. I could hear it and when I bent down I could feel the cold water with my fingers, but there was no light. I wasn't sure if I had gone blind, but then I looked up and could see the smallest shaft of light coming in through a hole in the ceiling. I washed my face in the stream and then decided to look around. It was almost impossible to make anything out and I had to feel my way around, hoping that there were no more holes to fall into.'

'It must have been very scary,' said Elspeth, feeling that she should say something.

'It was. I had no idea where I was, how I had got there or how I was going to get out. The floor seemed to be fairly solid, although in places it had a covering of peat. The walls were cold and seemed to be a mixture of earth and rock. The ceiling seemed to be mainly rock and was fairly low. I kept banging my head as I walked around. I found that the stream was coming out from under a huge boulder and then ran gently downhill. There was obviously only one way out of the cave and that was to follow the stream. I wasn't sure if I should stay were I was and hope that someone would come and find me, or whether I should try to find my own way out. Eventually I must have fallen asleep, because it was then I had the strangest dream. I seemed to be back on Weets with Dave and you were working on the picture. I could hear you telling us about how painting people captured their spirit and then I seemed to wake up. I sat there for some time trying to make sense of what had happened and then it dawned on me. If you had captured my spirit, why couldn't that spirit communicate with you? I then concentrated really hard and found that I could see Dave in his bed. It was amazing. It was as if I was there in the room with him. I tried to call to him, but I didn't seem to be able to shout out. Eventually I managed to say his name, but then the effort must have been too much because I passed out, or at least, fell asleep again.'

'That must have been last night, when I first

heard my name,' said Dave.

'That's right. I saw you sit up and look around the room, but then it all went black. When I woke up I decided to try again and that was just a little while ago. Now I seem to be able to speak to you quite easily and even walk around in this picture. It is really strange – I can touch the grass, but it feels like it is painted.'

Elspeth kept telling herself that this couldn't be real, but her senses were arguing with her. She could clearly see him and hear him. Why was she finding it so hard to accept? After all, it was she who had lived in the African bush and learned so much about the 'supernatural.' It was she who had told the kids about 'capturing the spirit' in a picture and it was she who had opened a shop in Pendle to sell spiritual artefacts. This was, however, the first time that she had really come face-to-face with anything that could truly be classed as 'mystical.' Sure, she had been to séances and sat around on Pendle Hill at the summer solstice with like-minded people all wanting to commune with other worlds. This was different. Part of her was terrified by what was happening, but by far the greater part was electrified with adrenaline and she had never felt so alive. All her life she had been waiting for something like this to happen.

'Where are you now?' she asked, deciding that it was time to try and find a solution to Jen's problem.

'Still in the cave,' he said.

'Don't move. I am going to call the police and explain what has happened. They will know what to do.'

'What exactly are you going to tell them, Gran?' asked Dave. 'Let's be fair, it's a pretty incredible story and you are known for being a little eccentric!'

Dave had a point. How was she going to explain this to Inspector Wilcox without sounding like a complete nutcase or without him thinking she had something to do with his disappearance? Now was no time to worry about what people thought of her, now was the time for action.

'Dave,' she said, 'you stay here with Jen and I will go and call Inspector Wilcox. Hopefully he will believe me enough to investigate.'

With that Elspeth headed downstairs to make the most important call of her life.

'Inspector Wilcox, please,' she said in her best telephone voice. 'Inspector Wilcox? Thank god I caught you. This is Elspeth, we met yesterday ... Good, you remember. What I am going to say now is going to seem pretty bizarre, but I need you to listen and to believe me. I know that the missing boy is Jensen and I know approximately where he is.'

Elspeth then gave the policeman a description of where she thought he was. There was silence on the other end of the phone.

'That's all very interesting,' said the Inspector when he finally spoke. 'I don't suppose you would like to tell me how you know all of this, would you?'

Elspeth had already expected this question.

'No, Inspector, I can't and even if I could, you wouldn't believe me.'

'Why don't you let me be the judge of that?'

She quickly had to decide whether to tell him or not. No point. There was no way that a trained policeman was going to accept her story. She had seen cases on the television where psychics had helped with investigations, so she decided to try that route.

'I'm sure you have already done some background checks on me since my visit yesterday and already know that I am regarded as something of a local 'attraction.' I realise that many folk around here think that I am a brick short of a chimney, but I can assure you that the information I have given you is correct and we need to act on it quickly. Jensen is OK, but he is cold and tired and doesn't know how to get out of where he is.'

'I hope you are right,' said the Inspector, 'but you have still not told me how you know this.'

'It came to me in a vision.'

'Do you often have visions?'

'No, this is the first one.' As soon as she had said it she wished she hadn't. How was she going to convince him now? Lying did not come easily to her.

'So this is your first vision and you expect me to take it all at face value?'

This seemed like a reasonable question. Elspeth really wasn't sure what to do next.

'What do you have to lose? You know he is missing and so do I. As far as I know, there has been no information on the news or in the press confirming the name of the boy. Either I was involved with his disappearance, which I can assure you I wasn't, or there has to be something in what I am saying.' Elspeth was sounding very much in charge. She wanted so much for the Inspector to believe her, but realised it was going to be a huge leap of faith on his part.

'Put yourself in my shoes,' replied Inspector Wilcox in that calm, reassuring manner that can only come from someone who has been around a long time and seen more than most. 'What have you told me that I can take as being fact? I have still not told you if it is Jensen and you are assuming it is. You have not been able to give me anything that I can verify and you expect me to rush out and start looking.'

He was right. The problem was if she told him the truth he would be even less likely to believe her.

'Unless you can give me anything more to go on,' he said, 'I'm afraid there is not going to be much I can do.'

Elspeth's heart sank. She understood completely his position but she just wanted to shake some sense in to him.

'Thank you, Inspector. You have my number and I would appreciate it if you would call me when you want my help in finding Jensen.' With that she hung up.

Obviously they were not going to get any help from the police, so it was up to her and Dave to help Jen. She ascended the stairs as if she was a twenty year old again, and burst back in to the room. Dave and Jen both turned to look at her.

'I'm afraid we are on our own, boys,' she said, trying to hide her disappointment. 'The first thing we should do is ring your parents, Jen, and tell them that you are OK.'

'I'm not sure that is a great idea,' said Jen looking back out from the painting. 'Mum is going to be pretty upset already and I'm not sure she will be any more receptive than the police. My dad will just think you are a nut – no offence – but he wouldn't be able to get his head around this. Facts and figures are his thing; he's an engineer at Rolls Royce. Not a great believer in anything he can't calculate; never has been.'

Elspeth thought for a moment. She could see Jen's point and certainly didn't want to upset his family any more than they must already be.

'OK,' she said decisively, 'get your coat, Dave, we're heading up Weets.'

'What about Jen?' asked Dave as he leapt to his feet, 'or at least Jen's picture. Do we bring it or leave it here?

Elspeth suddenly noticed that it had started raining.

'I think we had better leave it here,' she said. 'We wouldn't want it to get ruined in the rain. Who knows what would happen then.'

Before they left the room they had Jen explain exactly where he had been when he had fallen through into the cave. Elspeth was sure she knew where he meant, so she rushed to her room to get her bag, threw in a few essentials: food and water because he was bound to be starving and a torch so that she could see into the cave. She then went outside to the shed to get some rope. She didn't have much and it didn't look too strong, but she was sure it would do the trick.

Suitably provisioned, she and Dave set out along the path that seemed very familiar to both of them now. Once at the top stile, Elspeth motioned to Dave that they were going to head straight on rather than striking off toward the trig point on the right. After about a hundred yards, Elspeth stopped and looked over the dry stone wall on the left of the path.

'It has to be somewhere around here,' she said, pointing across the heather. 'Let's climb over and start looking.'

Elspeth was amazingly nimble for a lady of advancing years. She hopped down on the other side of the wall and then surveyed the moor, hoping to see something obvious.

'I'm guessing that Jen fell through a sink hole or something similar. Let's spread out and see if we can find one.'

Dave started running to and fro in the wet heather, the steadily falling rain soaking through his boots and trousers.

'Let's try and be a little more scientific about

this,' suggested his gran. 'I'll make a mark on the wall here,' and with that she tucked her scarf in under the top head stone, 'and we will walk away from the wall and then turn and come back, making sure we cover every inch.'

It made sense to Dave, who just wanted to get on with it. Walking about 20 feet apart, the small search party made its way up and down, all the time looking left and right for any signs of a cave in. After the third sweep, Elspeth went and retrieved her scarf so that she could re-mark their progress. Another three sweeps and all they had managed to achieve was being drenched to the bone. The rain had got steadily heavier and a mist now enshrouded the whole of the hill. Undaunted they carried on. Three more sweeps, another move of the scarf and Dave was beginning to get frustrated.

'Why can't we find anything?'

Elspeth wished she had a good answer. She too had expected to be able to find the place fairly easily. After all, how could you miss a new sink hole that was big enough to swallow a boy?

Time was passing and with it the strength of the two would-be rescuers. Eventually Elspeth said what they had both been thinking.

'There is nothing here.'

Dave looked at her with an obvious tear in his

eye which he quickly wiped away, pretending it was just rainwater dripping down his face.

'We need to get back and talk to Jen. See if he can give us a better idea of where he is.'

The trip back down was painful. Disappointment and the cold and wet of the early evening combined to make every step hard work. It was now starting to get dark, which only added to their frustration because they did not want Jen to have to spend another night out on his own.

Towards the bottom of the lane, however, they were reassured to see a line of people, all wearing green fluorescent jackets, walking towards them.

'It must be a search party,' said Dave, his spirits rising for the first time in many hours.

As they got closer, Elspeth whispered to him that it was not going to do any good talking to them about things and that they should concentrate on getting back as soon as possible.

'Evening Ma'am,' said the first of the party to reach them. 'Don't suppose you've seen a boy about his age up on the moor have you?' He was pointing at Dave.

'Sorry,' she replied, 'we haven't seen anyone. Is someone missing?'

'A local lad by the name of Jensen, been missing for a couple of days now.'

'We'll keep an eye out and let you know,' said Elspeth as she carried on walking down towards Barlick.

'So it definitely is him! I knew we weren't going crazy,' said Dave as he bounded along by the side of Elspeth.

'Remember,' said Elspeth, 'only one of us here is crazy, sorry, eccentric.'

Dave smiled. It was great that Gran could crack a joke at such a time and it came as light relief to what was otherwise a fairly tense moment.

As soon as they were in the back door, Dave flipped off his shoes and went running up to his room. Elspeth followed at a slightly more genteel pace, but with no less urgency. She was halfway up the stairs when she heard Dave scream.

'He's gone!'

When she entered his bedroom, he was standing holding the painting in both hands and appeared to be searching it for signs of life.

'He's not there any more. Look, there's only one character there now and it's me.'

Elspeth took the painting from her distraught grandson and looked carefully at every inch of the painting. He was right. No sign of Jensen.

Chapter 8

Dave was close to tears. Elspeth tried to console him but felt as equally helpless as he did.

'I'm sure he will be back,' she said reassuringly. 'He did say that he could only contact us when he sat and concentrated. You can't expect him to still be sitting there. We've been gone for hours.'

It certainly made sense to Dave, but it didn't make him feel any better.

'Why don't you go and dry your hair and then put on some clean clothes?'

She thought that giving him something to do would help take his mind off things. As he headed down to the bathroom she picked up the painting to give it another good look.

'Jen,' she whispered, 'can you hear me?'

It was too much to hope that it was going to be that easy and it wasn't. No reply. No reappearance of the second figure. With that, Elspeth carefully replaced the painting against the wall and went downstairs to her own bedroom. Dave finished drying his hair on the towel and carefully replaced it on the heated rail. He was sure he was going to need it again later, so wanted to ensure it was dry. Then, uncharacteristically, he picked up all his dirty, wet clothes and put them in the laundry basket. Checking to see that his Gran wasn't around, he then streaked back up the stairs as fast as his legs could carry him. The last thing he wanted was to be seen butt naked!

He quickly put on a clean pair of boxer shorts and scouted around for something dry to wear.

'Yo, Dave.'

His heart skipped a beat. It was Jen. He was back in the picture and calling to him. Dave turned while he was putting on his shirt and as soon as he looked at Jen he could see something was wrong.

'You've got to help me. The stream is getting bigger and I am having difficulty finding a dry place to stand.'

'It's been raining all afternoon,' explained Dave, 'I never thought about your stream. Let me get Gran.'

He ran to the top of the stairs and called down to Elspeth.

'Quick Gran, he's back and in trouble!'

Elspeth came barrelling out of her bedroom and charged up the stairs.

'The stream is getting bigger,' shouted Dave before she had made it to his room. 'We have to do something.'

'Jen, tell me again where you were when this all happened.'

Jen quickly explained once more everything he could remember about where he was when he first heard the grouse and then where he was when he had fallen through the ground.

'But that is exactly where we were looking,' said Elspeth, trying to contain her frustration. 'OK, for whatever reason, there is no sign of where the ground gave way, so we need to come up with a new plan. Jen, is there no way that you can climb back out where you came in?'

'No chance. There's only a small opening and the walls slope inwards, making it impossible to climb.'

'OK. You said the stream comes out under a big boulder. Is there any way you can follow the stream up beyond the boulder and out that way?'

'Nope,' came the immediate response. 'I've

already looked and the cave ends where the stream comes in.'

'Then you have no option but to follow the stream down and try to find a way out. We will stay here and wait for you to report back.'

Jen agreed that this was the best option and said he would be back to talk to them in half an hour at the latest. With that he disappeared from the painting again and started to make his way carefully along the stream, keeping one hand against the wall to keep himself steady and sliding his foot forward a little at a time to make sure there were no surprises waiting for him in the dark.

As soon as he had gone, Elspeth went downstairs to call Inspector Wilcox.

'One moment, please,' said the helpful lady at the station, 'I will patch you through to him now.'

'Hello, Inspector Wilcox here,' came the familiar voice.

'Hello, Inspector, it's Elspeth again. I understand that it is definitely Jen you are looking for. We bumped into your search team on Weets.'

'That's right,' he said almost apologetically. 'I hope you understand that I couldn't confirm the boy's identity to you earlier. I hope you are not feeling offended.'

'It doesn't matter how I feel,' said Elspeth, trying

not to sound too annoyed. 'The main thing is to get Jen back safe and sound. He is trapped underground and searching to find a way out. You need to get some caving experts up there quickly, and find a way in.'

There was no reply at the other end of the phone.

'Are you still there, Inspector?'

'You are not going to like this at all,' came the reply. 'I'm up on Weets now and we have just called the search off for the night as it's too dark to see anything. I cannot risk any of the search team getting injured. We will start again at first light. If there is any more hard information you can give me it would really help, but I need facts, Elspeth, solid facts.'

Elspeth hung up. She couldn't believe it; they were giving up the search. She made a cup of tea and a hot chocolate for Dave and decided not to tell either him or Jen about the phone call. They sat close to each other on the bed enjoying their hot drinks and wondering what Jen was up to. It didn't seem fair. They were warm and cosy in the light and poor Jen was feeling his way through a cold dark cave, fighting for his life. Neither said a word, they didn't need to. There was a bond between them now that would last for the rest of their lives.

Suddenly Jen was back in the painting.

'OK so far,' he said. 'The cave gets a little tight in places, but it seems to always widen again. I'll keep going and come back to you in a while. I must be getting somewhere,' he said, 'because the ground is starting to slope away pretty steeply now.'

Again he was gone. The pair on the bed looked at each other. There was nothing they could do except wait for Jen to return. Elspeth suggested that they both head for the kitchen and make themselves something to eat.

'What about the painting?'

'Bring it with you. I guess it's the picture Jen needs, not the bedroom.'

Dave grabbed the canvas and they made their way down to the kitchen.

'I think it's a nuggets and fries night, and then maybe a milkshake. What do you think?'

'Sounds great,' said Dave, 'but I can't help feeling guilty about Jen.'

'Your not eating isn't going to help him in the slightest. Just think, we may need to head out again at any time and having something in your belly will give you extra strength.'

This made Dave feel better because he really

was hungry and didn't want to miss out on nuggets and fries. He helped Elspeth when he could and stayed out of the way when he couldn't. He flipped between the kitchen and the lounge so that he could watch the local news and also listen to the local radio station. Both were carrying stories about Jen being missing, but neither had anything new to report. Basically there was not going to be anything new until tomorrow, given the fact that the search had finished for the night. Dave turned off the TV and sat down at the kitchen table. The painting was propped up on the worktop so that they would know as soon as Jen reappeared. Elspeth dished out two plates full of food and placed one in front of Dave. She slid the ketchup towards him and sat down opposite, ready to eat.

'Damn, that looks good. I hadn't realised how hungry I was until I saw that!' Jen was back. 'Nice kitchen.' He was filthy and looked soaking wet.

'Sorry,' said Dave and with an embarrassed smile he moved his plate out of Jen's sight. 'How's it going Jen?'

'Well,' he said in a considered manner, 'I'm still making progress, but the stream is getting bigger and the tunnel smaller. Some of the time I have to crawl along inside the water on my hands and knees because the ceiling is so low. It's really cold, but there is no alternative. It is getting really steep and there are parts now that I have to climb down, which is tough when you can't see where you are going or what you are doing.'

'Is it pretty much a straight line or are you having to change direction all the time?' asked Elspeth.

'Pretty straight,' replied Jen, 'Why.'

'I was just thinking about where you might be heading. If we know approximately where you started and you say you are heading downhill and in a straight line, you must be heading towards Salterforth or Foulridge. At least we know that much.'

'Good thinking,' said Jen.

Dave smiled.

'I'll be off,' said Jen, 'I don't like the way the stream is getting higher. I'll report back later.'

Elspeth got up and started looking through a kitchen drawer. Eventually she turned around, triumphantly holding a local map in her hand.

'Let's have a look and see if we can make some educated guesses as to where he might be.'

She laid the map out on the table and Dave returned to eating his meal now that he wasn't being watched.

'If he started out here,' said Elspeth pointing to

where they had been searching earlier, 'and he has been heading downhill for the last few hours, then he has to be somewhere around here,' and circled an area on the map.

'How does that help us?' asked Dave. 'He could be anywhere in that area.'

'At least it narrows it down and gives me an area to ask Inspector Wilcox to concentrate on in the morning,' replied Elspeth. 'Any help is better than none.'

Once again, Dave had to agree although it didn't make him feel any better.

The pair sat there for what seemed like ages. Eventually Elspeth suggested they move into the lounge so that they could be comfortable. She also thought it would be a good idea for Dave to watch some TV and keep his mind occupied. As usual there didn't seem to be much on and he kept flicking from one channel to another. Normally this would have driven Elspeth insane, but she sat there quietly and said nothing. Eventually Dave must have found something he liked, because the 'surfing' stopped. Elspeth wondered why he had decided on *House Doctor* but as she quite enjoyed it, she decided to say nothing. When the adverts came on she looked over at Dave and then understood. He was fast asleep with the remote in his hand. She smiled and settled down to watch part two.

The pair awoke with a start. They could hear Jen shouting for them from the kitchen. Elspeth glanced at the clock: 2.40am. They had both been asleep for about five hours.

'Jen,' called Dave, 'Jen what's the matter?'

'I'm scared and I'm trapped and I think I'm going to die!'

The words sent a chill down their spines.

'Calm down, Jen,' said Elspeth. 'Tell me what's going on.'

'The stream is now more like a river. It is nearly filling the whole tunnel. The last piece was so steep that I had to climb down what was basically a waterfall. Halfway down I slipped and fell into a small lake where the water is gathering. When I looked around there was no way out. I tried to climb back up the stream, but it was too slippery. Then I heard an awful crashing noise and the roof started to cave in. The tunnel is blocked. The rain has brought the roof down and I can't get back the way I came. The water is still coming in and there is nowhere to go. What can I do?'

For the first time, Jen sounded like a scared little boy rather than a confident young man. Elspeth's heart went out to him. Dave just sat there stunned.

Think Elspeth, think. What can he do now? Elspeth was running through as many ideas as she could.

'Are you sure there is no other way out?'

'Certain.'

'Are you sure there is no way you can make it back up the tunnel?'

'Positive. I have already climbed back up as far as I can and the whole tunnel is blocked by the fallen ceiling.'

'How deep is the water?'

'Haven't tried it yet.'

'Before you do, can you swim?'

'Yep, no worries there. Just give me a minute.'

Jen left the picture and then re-appeared a couple of minutes later.

'It's only about waist deep,' he said, 'but it's getting deeper all the time.'

'I want you to walk back in and slide your hand along the roof of the tunnel where it meets the water. We need to know if there is a way out through the water. See if you can feel an air pocket or anything like that.'

Jen left again. This time he was gone for what seemed like an age, but which was, in reality, only about two minutes. When he returned he was soaking wet from top to toe.

'There is a way out,' he said and the pair sighed with relief. 'but it's blocked.'

'Blocked how?' asked Elspeth.

'There seems to be a grid across the exit and it's made of thick metal bars.'

Elspeth said nothing, but Dave could see that her mind was in overdrive. Quick as a flash she started pouring over the map that they had just been looking at.

'Here,' she said, 'he has to be here.'

Elspeth was pointing at an area of blue on the map.

'It is the only place where logically he can have come out. Whitemoor Reservoir. It is between the top of Weets and Foulridge and it makes sense that the underground stream would end up there. It has to be.'

'What now?' asked Jen trying to hide the terror that was in his voice. He was no longer able to find any dry area to stand on and the water was over his shoes and up to his ankles.

'I've got an idea,' said Elspeth, 'but you are going to have to be brave. Dave get ready, we are going out. Find a big plastic bag from under the sink and wrap up the painting, we're taking Jen with us.'

Dave had a purpose again and he jumped to

every order that Elspeth gave, just happy to be active. While he was doing that, Elspeth rang the police again.

'I'm sorry,' said the officer at the other end, 'you have come through to central comms and I cannot put you through to Inspector Wilcox. Is it an emergency or can it wait until morning?'

Elspeth slammed the receiver down in disgust.

'Jen,' she shouted, 'what's your home telephone number?'

With shaking hands she dialled the numbers as Jen called them out.

'Hello, is that Jensen's mother? You don't know me, but I live in Barlick and my name is Elspeth.'

'What do you think you are doing?' came a reply in a voice she wasn't expecting.

'Inspector Wilcox, I am I glad I found you. Get over to Whitemoor Reservoir immediately. I think we have found Jen.'

'Elspeth, I don't know what you think you are up to, but you should not have called here.'

In the background Elspeth could hear an hysterical woman crying. She had obviously heard what Elspeth had said and was shouting at Inspector Wilcox, demanding an explanation. He had obviously put the receiver down, but missed the cradle. Elspeth could hear every word of the conversation. Inspector Wilcox was trying to explain that Elspeth was a local crank who believed she had seen Jen in a vision. Jen's mother was prepared to believe anyone who might have good news and said she wanted to talk to her. Then what must have been Jen's dad joined in saying that he wasn't going to have some local lunatic upsetting his wife and told Inspector Wilcox to press charges. The whole place was in chaos. Elspeth hung up. She had only meant to help and felt guilty that she had made things worse. Still, time was passing.

Dave was waiting in the kitchen and after grabbing her coat and keys the pair headed out, Dave carrying Jen under one arm. Dave didn't even know that his Gran had a car, but two minutes later he was sitting in it. He had never been in one so old, but that was the least of his concerns. Elspeth didn't even bother to close the garage door as they drove off down the road. She was a woman on a mission.

'Are you still OK, Jen?' she asked as they headed up past Bancroft Mill.

'I'm OK for now,' he said, 'but please be quick. The water is rising at a hell of a rate.'

'Hold on, Jen, we're on our way.'

Truthfully she didn't know what they were going to do when they got there, but at least they were doing something.

The little green Morris Minor fought its way up the hill past Letcliffe Park and wound its way along the back road towards Barrowford. There was no traffic out, apart from them, which was no surprise given the time. The Fanny Grey pub flashed by on the right-hand side and Dave marvelled at how nippy the little car was. In fact they were hardly touching 30 mph, but the narrow road and high walls gave the impression of much greater speed.

'We're here,' shouted Elspeth as she pulled the car over to the side of the road.

Dave looked up and saw a large white sign with the name of the reservoir in big black letters.

'Come on,' called Elspeth who was already out of the car and halfway across the road.

Dave scrambled to keep up with her, but was struggling trying to carry the painting as well. At least it had now stopped raining which was a good omen, he thought to himself. Elspeth was halfway up the steep bank that separated the reservoir from the road. She kept slipping backwards due to the ground being so wet under foot, but gradually she made her way to the top. Dave joined her moments later, panting, but in one piece and with Jen firmly in tow.

'Now what?' he asked, looking to Elspeth for

more instructions.

'I have no idea. Let me think.'

Elspeth looked around, hoping for inspiration. The clouds that had been dropping so much water had now dispersed and the moon was casting a warm glow over the lake. Nothing. All she could see was water and the retaining walls.

'If he has come down from the hill, he has to be somewhere on the back side of the reservoir,' she thought to herself. 'If the water is building up around him, it has to be at the same level as the lake, so he must be somewhere just the other side of the retaining wall where it meets the hill.' All this seemed logical, but what could they do?

'Jen, can you give us any more detail about where you are?'

No reply. Dave ripped the carrier bag off the painting and to his horror Jen had gone.

'Jen! Can you hear me, Jen!' he shouted at the empty canvas.

Suddenly Jen reappeared.

'You have got to help me now,' he said. 'The water is up to my chest and my head is against the ceiling. The water is pouring in and there is nowhere to go. I don't know how much longer I can hold on.'

Elspeth looked left and right.

'What are you looking for, Gran?' asked Dave, desperate to help.

'A sluice of some sort. There has to be a way to drain the reservoir.'

Dave leapt in to action, leaving Elspeth's canvas lying on the ground at her feet. He darted along the edge of the reservoir, desperate to find anything that might resemble a drain point of some sort. Suddenly it was right in front of him; a huge wheel atop a worm screw. He shouted back to Elspeth to come and help him. She stooped to pick up Jen and then ran along to where Dave was already trying to turn the wheel.

'Hold on,' she shouted, not really sure if she was talking to Jen or Dave.

She grabbed the wheel alongside Dave and heaved with all her might.

'Please be quick, the water is nearly over my head, I've got nowhere to go.'

Spurred on by these words, Dave and Elspeth put one almighty effort into moving the wheel. Nothing. It would not budge an inch.

'Again,' shouted Elspeth and one more time the pair made a Herculean effort to move it – but to no avail. They could hear Jen starting to scream from the painting. Dave was looking at Elspeth, willing her to magic a solution to their problem, but she was completely out of ideas. They couldn't come this close and then let Jen die.

'You had better be right, this could cost me my job.'

Inspector Wilcox had appeared from nowhere and was leaning into the sluice wheel with all his might. Dave leapt to his side and Elspeth shouted for joy as she added her weight and felt the wheel start to move. Below them she could hear the rush of water as it forced its way out from the bottom of the sluice gate.

'Hold on, Jen,' she shouted, 'the water level is going to drop.'

Inspector Wilcox looked at the pair of them in total amazement. There was no one there for them to be talking to and yet they both seemed elated. He carried on turning the wheel, wondering how on earth he was going to explain this one in his report. The water was now gushing out of the sluice and into the drainage channel that would eventually take it down to Foulridge. When the gate could be opened no more Elspeth and Dave hugged each other and then hugged the Inspector.

Dave picked up the painting and panicked when he realised Jen was nowhere in sight. He shouted Jen's name over and over again but to no avail. Elspeth stared at him. Inspector Wilcox stared at both of them. He had no idea what was going on. Dave had gone from being ecstatic to being totally overwhelmed in the blink of an eye. They were too late. They had been so close to saving him and yet they had failed him at the last minute. Dave sunk to his knees and started to sob. Elspeth tried to console him, but that was going to be impossible. She held him close, so close that she was afraid she would hurt him. Dave cried with such deep pain that his whole body shook with emotion.

Inspector Wilcox looked at the pair of them and, while not knowing what on earth was going on, he knew that this was a private moment, one that he should not intrude upon, so he quietly slipped off in to the darkness.

Elspeth and Dave stayed locked together, sharing the grief of not only losing a friend, but of losing a friend that they felt sure they could have saved. Losing a friend that they had let down in his hour of need. Surely nothing could feel worse than this?

Eventually Elspeth managed to get Dave to his feet. He was clinging on to the painting as if it had been Jen himself. She gently steered him along the edge of the reservoir and towards Whinberry Boathouse, where they could more easily climb down from the raised walls without slipping.

As they reached the steps, they both turned and

looked back across the black surface of the lake. It was a strangely peaceful scene, yet none the less a cruel one, knowing as they did that a young life had been needlessly extinguished that night. The wind was blowing gently and carried with it the sounds of the night; the rustling of the trees, the call of an owl as it hunted for prey and the stirring of the livestock in the next field. There was something else, too. It sounded like Elspeth's name.

They first looked at each other and then at the painting. It had to be Jen. The moon shone bright enough for them to pick out every detail in the picture. No Jen.

There it was again. It was Inspector Wilcox!

'You are a bloody marvel,' he said rushing up to Elspeth and planting a huge kiss on her cheek. 'A bloody marvel, that's what you are.'

He was grinning from ear to ear.

'I don't know what you did or how you did it, but he's alive. Come on, he's calling for you,' and with that he grabbed them both by the hand and towed them around to the back of the reservoir. Dave immediately leapt into the water and found the top of the grate. He couldn't see Jen, but he could hear him and, more to the point, he could see his hand sticking out from between the bars. Dave reached forward and grabbed it, feeling how cold it had become.

'Hang on, Jen,' he shouted, 'We're coming.'

The rest of the night passed in total chaos. Inspector Wilcox organised an ambulance, some divers with heavy cutting equipment, the arrival of Jen's parents, journalists, warm blankets and hot tea. It was amazing to watch. The water level dropped to the point where everyone could see Jen and the divers cutting away the bars. Jen was reunited firstly with his parents and then with Dave and Elspeth before being taken off to hospital. 'Thank You's were being said all around and there were hugs and kisses for everyone.

'Well done, Elspeth, well done, Dave.'

The pair looked up to see who had said the words they must have heard a hundred times that night. They had not recognised the voice and now they could see the person, they did not recognise them either.

'Thank you,' said Elspeth, polite as always, 'We were just glad to help.'

'You should both be very proud. I have been watching your progress Elspeth, ever since you arrived in Barlick. While people mock you, you smile with an inner peace. When people question you, you answer with a calm and confident manner. When destiny called, you acted without thought.

You and I will meet again Elspeth, maybe not soon, but we will meet again.'

Elspeth and Dave looked at the woman. She had an air about her – something special, they just couldn't quite work out what – that separated her from the crowd. She smiled.

'I'm sorry,' said Elspeth, 'I know it sounds rude, but who are you?'

'My friends call me Maggie. My given name is Margaret Rose Pendle. The Hill Folk around here know me as Midnight Rose,' and with that she turned and vanished in to the darkness.

'I guess we will just notch that up to yet another bizarre moment in an amazingly bizarre day,' she said, looking at Dave. Deep down, however, she knew she would see Maggie again.

Eventually the circus departed and Elspeth and Dave made their way back to Barlick in her little old car.

'I thought we had lost him,' said Dave as they dropped down Tubber Hill towards town.

'Me too,' said Elspeth. 'I guess the painting only worked when he really needed us. As soon as the water went down enough for him to be out of danger, his captured spirit returned to him, knowing he had the greater need.'

Once again, it made sense. What an amazing

woman his grandmother was.

They put the car in the garage and made their way back to the house. It was now early morning and the sun was starting to come up. Dave and Elspeth had promised to see Jen later in the day and the police had said they also needed to see them. They had to decide by then what they were going to tell Inspector Wilcox!

Having taken off their shoes, they both wandered through to the lounge where they collapsed into their easy chairs, both sighing as they did so.

Closing her eyes, Elspeth smiled to herself. The last 24 hours had been amazing. Dave had been amazing. She could not have been prouder than she felt that moment.

'Elspeth.'

'Elspeth, please help.'

'Elspeth, over here.'

Her eyes snapped open. All around her were paintings calling to her from the walls of her lounge.

'I have always included people in my paintings ever since I lived in Africa ...'

Part Three
Sandy's Journey

Chapter 1

The first week of September already. Sandy couldn't believe it. The summer holidays seemed a distant memory now as she looked down at the canal from bridge number 151 outside the Anchor public house at Salterforth.

No boats were moving on the famous Leeds and Liverpool Canal this morning, just a few ducks. What had once been a proud waterway, one of the mainstays of the British industrial scene teeming with cargo, was now effectively relegated to day trippers and tourism. The whole system was undergoing regeneration, but it was never going to return to its glory days of the 19th and early 20th centuries.

A number of people still lived fulltime on the canal, lined up along the banks on temporary moorings or more permanently at marinas such as Lower Park in Barnoldswick. Few people, however, managed to make a good living from the water anymore.

Sandy sighed; time to get moving. She checked her watch, shouldered her new book bag and made her way off the bridge to join the towpath.

The walk along to West Craven High Technology College was not a bad way to start the day, she thought, or at least it wasn't on a day like this. The early morning sun was glistening through drops of dew hanging off the ends of branches overhanging the path and was causing those sitting on the tips of the emerald green blades of grass which hedged the cinder track to sparkle.

The canal itself seemed to steam under the warming rays of the early sunlight, fighting their way through the long shadows cast by the dry stone walls and vegetation that followed the canal along its 127 mile length. A similar story had been played out each bright morning since the canal had been built in the 18th century. Sandy loved to hear stories of the early days of the canal and her favourite was of how, in 1912, a cow called Buttercup fell into the canal and swam the entire length of the Foulridge tunnel, before being dragged out and revived with brandy. 'Wonder if that is where Brandy Butter originated?' she thought to herself with a wry smile.

Making her way through the car park, Sandy stopped and opened the door of a small stone-built pillar that stood alongside the canal bank. Inside, she knew, was a tap which she turned with one hand, cupping the other under the free flowing water which pooled in her now-chilled fingers. She raised her hand and drank deeply, as she had done many times that summer since moving to Salter-forth. She had found the tap by accident one day while out exploring. On reflection it was no great surprise, as it was there as a source of fresh water for the boats that made their way up and down the canal and in particular for those that were moored up close by. She, however, preferred to think of it as her personal fountain of life's precious elixir, for those days when she was caught in the middle of the Sahara, or halfway up Mount Kilimanjaro, even though it was only a few hundred yards from her house.

Wiping her mouth on the back of her hand, she checked her watch again. It was as if she didn't really want to start her journey to school in earnest. Sandy felt as if every year she was starting afresh at a new school. She had lost track of how many she had attended in her short life and tried to remember the name of her last school, but honestly couldn't. She stood up straight, looked along the path and told herself that this year was going to be different. This year she was going to make friends. This year she was going to be picked for the netball team. This year was going to be the beginning of the rest of her life.

'I'm really sorry!'

That was all Sandy could hear as she was broadsided by something, someone, probably. She had been looking down over the park watching a spaniel charging aimlessly round in circles when she was suddenly hit by a force strong enough to not only knock her off her feet, but to knock her clean off the path and into the undergrowth.

She felt a hand reach out to grab her and then she was being lifted unceremoniously to her feet. While regaining her composure, she felt a rather strange sensation around her ankles. Sandy looked down to see a Bedlington Terrier sniffing and licking her legs. She relaxed.

'Really sorry about that,' said a girl, probably three years Sandy's senior, 'Should have looked before jumping off the boat. I'm Esther, by the way, and that is Ellen.'

The girl was pointing back across the path at a girl who was still standing on the bow of a beautifully painted narrowboat. Her head was in her hands and she was gently shaking it from side to side.

'How many times have I told you to look before you leap?' she said, the question obviously being levied at Esther.

'I know, you'd think I'd learn,' she replied with a big beaming grin. 'Anyway, you OK?'

Sandy was brushing leaves and dew off her skirt.

'No harm done,' she said, 'nothing broken.'

'Excellent!' said Esther. 'See, no problems here,' and she flashed a grin back at Ellen before hurtling off down the towpath.

Ellen sprung down to the track and held out her hand to Sandy.

'Ellen,' she said, 'pleased to meet you.'

Sandy took her hand and shook it warmly, pleased to have met someone close to her own age.

'Sandy,' she said 'and the pleasure is all mine. Do you guys live on the boat?'

'Yep,' came the reply, 'have done for a few years now.'

They started to walk together while Esther had already raced ahead with the dog. As they reached the last window which looked through to the galley, Ellen waved to an older man who was sitting reading his paper and supping a brew. He didn't move a muscle, too caught up in the news of the day to acknowledge the gesture.

'He's great,' said Ellen. 'Never questions what we

get up to, just leaves us to get on with things really. By the way, that's Boo.'

'Who, your dad?' asked Sandy, somewhat surprised at the way Ellen had referred to her father.

'No, dummy – the dog is called Boo.'

Both girls started laughing. It was nice to share a joke with someone, thought Sandy, after having entertained herself for most of the summer.

They caught up with Esther and Boo quite quickly, as they were both looking at something down in the flood sluice by the side of the canal. It was a dead rabbit as it turned out, obviously left by a fox the night before.

'This your first year at West Craven?' asked Esther, looking at Sandy's clean blazer.

Sandy tried to look confident. 'Certainly is, and I'm looking forward to it.'

'Don't,' came the reply, 'you are going to hate it. I can't wait to get out.'

'Shut up, Esther,' shouted Ellen. 'Don't take any notice of her. It's fine, as schools go. I'm sure you're going to fit right in. She just can't wait to leave and go to Nelson and Colne College, thinks school is for kids. It's our last year, with any luck, and then we're off to college to do our A levels.'

Sandy tried to smile, but she certainly didn't feel any more confident after those encouraging words from the girls!

'I'm sure we will see you around school' said Ellen breezily.

'But we obviously won't speak to you,' Esther chipped in 'because we are seniors and you are just starting. Just not done, you understand.'

She said it in such a matter of fact manner that Sandy didn't take any offence, just stored it away as a helpful piece of information for future use.

The three of them, four if you count Boo, set off and quickly passed under bridge 151a, the newest bridge in the area which carried the main Kelbrook Road into Barnoldswick.

'Duck!' bellowed Esther suddenly, when they were halfway under.

It was so loud and so unexpected that Sandy's heart nearly stopped.

'Don't pay any attention to her,' said Ellen, seeing the look on Sandy's face. 'She thinks it's funny, as the sound gets amplified under here and echoes.'

'She wasn't wrong,' thought Sandy, her nerves slightly less on edge now. By the time they had cleared the short tunnel Sandy actually thought it was quite funny and decided she would do the same to some other unsuspecting victim when the opportunity arose. A tradition worth continuing.

The four new amigos chatted about this and that, nothing in particular, but conversation flowed easily. Esther and Boo kept disappearing into the hedges or through the wall whenever possible, hunting down who knows what and coming back with an interesting 'thing' they had found.

They stopped to look across the canal to the open fields where rabbits seemed in abundance and geese could be heard honking. Closer to them, in fact just up on the opposite bank, was a family of swans.

'Seven cygnets,' said Esther, guessing that Sandy was trying to count them. 'Not a single one lost since they hatched.'

Often the local pike or mink helped themselves to a duckling or two and it was rare for any of the mallards that lived on this stretch of canal to keep an entire brood. It seemed cruel, but it was, after all, just nature's way of keeping the balance.

As soon as the swans had spotted them, they launched themselves majestically into the water and traversed the canal like a flotilla at a royal event. The cob took the lead to protect his family and the pen brought up the rear. The brood was sandwiched in between doting parents who wanted to see what these people might have to offer in the way of food and to be sure they should let their offspring eat it. Sadly for them, none of the children had brought anything that morning. Sandy made a mental note to bring some bread the next day so that she could get to know them better.

Having found out that their efforts had been in vain, the cob hissed at the group, raising himself menacingly out of the water and then turned to lead his family back to the bank where they waddled out, slightly less gracefully then their entrance, to continue their morning preening session.

The girls turned, waving goodbye to the uninterested swans and made their way towards Cockshott Bridge, number 152. All the bridges along the canals were numbered so as to help the boats with navigation and timings. Sometimes bridges were removed, without changing the numbers of those that stayed, confusing to those new to the water. When bridges were added, letters were used, like the 151a Kelbrook Road Bridge, so as not to interrupt the numbering that had been in place for hundreds of years.

Cockshott Bridge was a grade two listed building, as far as the planning office was concerned. It stood unassumingly at the south end of the marina at Lower Park in Barnoldswick – or 'Barlick' as it was known locally – and provided access from the main road to the canal path and further across the fields to join with Ben Lane, an unadopted road linking Salterforth with the Thornton end of Barlick.

The girls stood atop the construction, looking down at the marina shop, a favourite with the kids at West Craven. A steady stream of blazers could be seen every lunch break as they made their way across the playing fields and down the road to buy sweets and other contraband, carelessly discarding wrappers into the hedgerows and returning quickly to ensure they were back before afternoon lessons started.

Sandy's heart missed a beat. The school was now in sight and she was minutes away from starting yet another term, a term she hoped would be like no other she had yet experienced.

Chapter 2

Everywhere she looked there were kids running. Kids running in the car park, kids running in the hallways, kids running in the playground, just kids running.

It was all a little overwhelming. There had probably been an open day when new pupils could come and see what the school had to offer and where their new classrooms were going to be, but Sandy had missed that. Something she was now beginning to regret. She looked around, trying to get her bearings and trying to glean some insight as to where she should be.

Esther and Ellen were long gone. They had disappeared into the mass of bodies flowing through the hallways, like blood through arteries, as soon as they had set foot in the building.

Panic set in. The clock was ticking and she didn't want to be late to her first lesson or meeting her home room teacher, whichever was supposed to happen first. Sandy saw a group of wide-eyed, pale-faced young students looking just as lost as her and decided it was a good place to start. As she arrived to join the morass, a woman walked out from a door marked 'Staff Only' with a piece of paper in her hand.

'OK,' shouted the woman, 'for all those of you who are lost, here are the form room numbers. If you are not sure which form you are in, why not? We sent you a letter which you should now have with you.'

Sandy froze. What letter? Had she had a letter and forgotten about it? She didn't remember receiving anything from the school and she certainly didn't have anything in her book bag to shed any light on where she should go.

'Registration begins at 08:50, don't be late to your rooms. Year Sevens in particular be sure to get to where you should be, we don't want to have to explain to parents how we lost their bright young things before we've even begun your education!'

Everyone started scattering in all directions. Sandy chose the one that most people were running in and joined the throng. Round two corners she raced, trying not to collide with older kids who were looking at them with a knowing smile on their faces. They had all been through it, part of the rites of passage, to be hated when it happened to you and to be savoured when you watched! One more corner and into a room where there were already a number of smug-looking individuals sitting at desks.

'I bet they have their letters,' thought Sandy to herself as she scanned the room to look firstly at the faces and then secondly for empty desks. She wasn't alone in what she was doing and although she lunged for a desk near the window, a tall pimply faced youth slumped himself down in 'her' chair before she could claim it. Her second choice went the same way. It didn't seem to matter which way she turned, someone got there first.

Suddenly a voice boomed out from behind her.

'Find a chair and sit in it before you end up standing in the corridor for the rest of the day, or the rest of the term if I decide I don't like you!'

Sandy felt a lump appear in her throat. She looked around. Just four desks remaining as far as she could see and only three people left standing. With a feeling of complete exhaustion and relief she parked herself in the nearest space and let her book bag slip to the floor.

'My name is Mr Anderson and I am probably the most universally hated teacher at the school. I have drawn the short straw this year and have to teach you rabble, so let me impart the rules of engagement. You do as I say, when I say it, without question. You have your work in on time and complete. You do not, under any circumstances, talk during my lessons, unless it is to me, after you have raised your hand and after I have told you to speak. Remember these simple rules and you will live to reach year 8.'

Sandy looked around, trying to gauge others' reactions, but all eyes were on Mr Anderson. He was a legend at the school, but not in a good way, at least as far as the kids were concerned. Parents often saw it differently and many actually reminisced about the good old days and a return to discipline. This year, as every year, saw a class full of shell-shocked pupils not knowing what to do, and most of them had stopped breathing for fear of retribution.

Sandy looked over at the classroom door and saw two familiar faces beaming through the glass. Esther and Ellen smiled, gave the thumbs up and then disappeared from view. 'Esther was right,' seemed to echo through Sandy's brain and she braced herself for the term ahead.

The rest of the morning seemed to pass without too much trauma. One lesson seemed to flow into the next, as new books were handed out, names taken and homework dispensed. Lunchtime was spent looking around the yard and the field and trying to memorise the layout of the school and classrooms. It seemed like no sooner had it started than the bell was sounding and Sandy was back inside for English. She had developed a system for remaining relatively invisible; she had found this to be a great survival technique for new schools. She sat quietly, never put her hand up unless most people had theirs up. Safety in numbers, she thought, and you would never find her talking to anyone at adjacent desks.

'Who wants to explain the pluperfect tense?'

Sandy looked at her desk, not wanting to engage any eye contact with the teacher.

'How about you at the back?'

Sandy's eyes stayed resolutely downward.

'Are you deaf, child, and blind? I am talking to you.'

Sandy could feel her temperature rising, her face was going red and beads of perspiration were forming on her brow, but still she didn't look up. She heard footsteps coming closer. Her knuckles gripped the side of the desk and she wished she could just disappear. She had no idea what the answer was and she certainly wasn't ready to be embarrassed in front of her new class on the first day of school. She could see shoes now on the floor by the side of her desk leg.

'I am talking to you. There is little point in just looking at your desk aimlessly hoping I will go away, because let me assure you I won't.'

Sandy's blood had run cold and she realised there was nothing else for it. She looked up, ready to speak, but instead of being eyeballed by a rampaging bull of a teacher, she saw the back of his head, leaning over the next desk to hers.

'Are you deaf as well as stupid, boy?'

Music to Sandy's ears. That phrase, one heard by countless pupils in countless schools through the ages, told her that she had once again escaped public castigation. She outwardly breathed a sigh of relief, not feeling in the slightest bit sorry for the recipient of the outburst, nor guilty about feeling that way.

By the time the last lesson drew to a close, Sandy was definitely ready to head homeward. She had managed another first day without incident. OK, she hadn't made any friends, but there was plenty of time for that another day. The main thing was it hadn't been nearly as bad as she had expected, given Esther's pep talk earlier that morning! The bell sounded and the classroom filled with the sound of chair legs dragging along the floor and desk tops being closed. The teacher's voice was being drowned out by the excited chatter of the new intake, all eager to exchange stories about how bad the first day had been and how they had so nearly ended up in detention, even though they hadn't. Sandy smiled. She could now. She was remembering how similar this scene was to her first day last year.

She grabbed her bag and headed out into the corridor, hoping to catch sight of the girls. Not surprisingly they were nowhere to be seen. Sandy cut through the back field and picked up the marina road that ran down to the canal. There was, as ever, a gentle buzz of activity at the marina. The pace of life on the water was slower than elsewhere. Rarely did people rush around and rarely did they look stressed. Three or four people were sitting on benches, nursing cups of coffee and judging the capabilities of the various boats being steered past the ones that were moored up. There was not a great deal of space to manoeuvre when the canal was lined by boats on both banks, but it was unusual for any collisions to take place, although not unheard of. Others were out washing decks and hulls, while yet more were weeding small portable flowerbeds grown in buckets and pots along their roofs. It was amazing, the ingenuity of people, she thought, seeing tomato plants bursting out of a growbag on the stern of one particularly beautifully painted narrowboat.

Sandy stood for a while on the bridge, watching the general comings and goings before deciding to wander home. Secretly she had been hoping that the girls would appear and that they could walk back together, but that was obviously not going to happen.

Expectant ducks took turns at shadowing her along the path, all hoping that she would suddenly produce bread from her bag and when they realised that this was unlikely, they dropped off, only to be replaced by other optimistic quacking friends. Dragonflies and damselflies flitted from reed to reed accompanied by a glorious song provided by two robins either talking to, or trying to out-sing the other – difficult to tell which. Fieldfares sat in the hawthorn trees and bluetits darted here and there picking caterpillars off the nettles. It truly was a magical place when you took the time to see what was there. 'So many people are in too much of a hurry to notice all the little things that are there to be cherished,' thought Sandy as she heard two cars racing each other down Kelbrook Road. Life is too short not to squeeze every last experience out of it.

As she exited the road bridge, she nearly collided with a lady jogging with a small child in a buggy. It was one of those three-wheeled buggies that looked like it had been designed by someone who thought they were building a four-wheel-drive off-road vehicle. Sandy just managed to jump to one side, avoiding the guaranteed collision of shins and wheels.

'I'm really sorry,' shouted the jogger as she came to a halt and turned to face Sandy. It's amazing how people with iPods always shout, thought Sandy. Val took her earpieces out and then spoke in a more normal volume.

'I didn't hear you coming,' she smiled, 'that's the downside of these things,' pointing at the MP3 player strapped to her arm. 'I really am sorry,' she said again and it was quite obvious she meant it.

'No problem,' replied Sandy, who by now had had time to look at the cute little boy in the buggy. She bent down and smiled at him and was immediately greeted by the biggest grin Sandy could ever remember having seen.

'He's a happy one, that's for sure,' said Val, proud of that fact that her son greeted people with the same non-judgmental expression that most red setters use.

Sandy beamed back at him. 'He certainly is a keeper.'

Val laughed. 'You don't really get a choice.'

Sandy suddenly felt foolish, but she had meant it as a joke.

'But I know exactly what you mean, thanks,'

and she flashed a wide grin at Sandy. 'Do you live around here?'

'Just along the canal at Salterforth,' Sandy replied, delighted that someone was taking notice of her.

'I'm surprised that I haven't seen you before,' said Val, 'as I run along here most days with Matt.'

'I'll keep an eye out for you in future,' said Sandy as she rose to her feet.

'Well, must keep the muscles warm,' and with that Val took off along the towpath, pushing the buggy with one hand, and trying to wave goodbye and replace the earpieces of her iPod, all at the same time.

Sandy smiled. 'It's been a good day,' she thought to herself. 'Hopefully two, no, three friends made, four if you count Boo.' A new term, a new start, that is what she had wanted and if today was anything to go by, that was what she was going to get.

Chapter 3

Sandy rose early. She wasn't sure if it was a carry-over from yesterday's excitement or just because the sun seemed particularly bright this morning.

Every now and then there are mornings when the air seems crystal clear and the sky an intense azure blue. It is as if everything comes into focus, as if someone has cleaned the windows in your house and there is no dust in the atmosphere. Anyway, it meant she was on the canal bank early, hoping to catch up with Esther and Ellen again. She wondered how she was going to be able to hang around so she could see them coming off their boat, but without looking desperate. We have all been there, wanting something badly, but not wanting to be seen wanting it. Stupid really, but people are strange like that. It all comes down to embarrassment, a much over-rated and usually unnecessary emotion. Thankfully most people outgrow it, eventually.

She decided to walk under the bridge at the Anchor this morning, to see if there were any fish or ducks to look at. She trailed her hand along the stones in the wall and felt her fingers slip into the grooves that had been cut by years of use. 'If only they could tell their story,' she thought to herself. These grooves had been worn in the stone through years of rope friction. When the barges had been pulled by horse, before being replaced by engines, the tow ropes used to get caught on trees, walls and bridges, wherever there was a tight bend, like there was under the bridge at Salterforth. The horses turned through the bend before the barges got to the apex and consequently the ropes rubbed on the corners of the stone blocks in the bridge. As most horses used were about the same size – huge – the ropes always rubbed at the same point, eventually creating a groove. The big problem with this was that the ropes got frayed and they snapped when under tension, often causing the barge to drift off into the path of another boat. In an attempt to stop this happening, rollers were sometimes put in place, exactly like the ones that Sandy was now running her hands over. At the entrance and exit to the bridge – both the same, really, as it just depends on which direction you are traveling – vertical rollers had been installed along the path. The idea was that they took the strain of the ropes, rather than the stones. Not only was the roller made of wood and therefore much gentler on the rope than the harsh, coarse surface of the rock, but they also rotated as the rope was pulled over them by the horse. This saved the rope, put less strain on the harness of the horse and helped the boat to turn by making the journey through the bend a gentler one. It made the horse's job easier as well. There were small grooves cut into the wooden rollers too, but overall there was considerably less wear and tear all round.

Sandy was gently spinning the rollers without even realising what she was doing, as her mind was preoccupied watching for the girls. No sign. She checked her watch. She had better make a move or risk being late, not good on only your second day.

As she passed their boat, she was greeted by a broadside from Boo who deftly leapt from the stern, a whoop of delight from Esther who hurled herself from inside the cabin, having been waiting for Sandy to walk by and a more genteel 'Good morning' from Ellen.

Sandy grinned, this was just what she had been

hoping for but had feared was a one-off.

'Thought you'd never get here,' laughed Esther 'We've been waiting for ages.'

All smiles, they set off, stopping briefly to wave in through the cabin window at the outline of the figure reading the paper. Boo skipped obediently along behind them.

'Try outs for netball today,' said Esther without looking at either of them.

Sandy wasn't sure if the comment was aimed at her or Ellen.

'Do you play netball?'

Now Sandy realised it must be her she was talking to.

'Have done in the past,' she replied, not wanting to brag about the fact that she had played for the school team, but hoping someone would ask for clarification. She thought she was good enough to play for the county side, but had never really stayed anywhere long enough to establish herself.

'Give it a go, then. Trials are at 4pm immediately after school on the netball court in the yard.'

This gave Sandy something to look forward to. Her kit was already at school and this was going to be an opportunity to make even more friends. It annoyed her that she still couldn't find any of the paperwork the school was supposed to have sent her, because she was sure that things like the trials would have been mentioned on the calendar, but she was just happy that she now knew it was on.

The farmers were out early that day and they were already taking the first cut of silage from the fields by the river. This was much to the annoyance of the rabbits that were scattering in all directions as the vibrating blades made quick work of the grass. Generally this scene was played out three times a year, each time the grass grew about as tall as the rabbit's ears when they stood on their back legs. Sandy felt sure this wasn't actually how the farmers gauged when to cut it, but it did seem like a reasonable rule of thumb. Sadly, sometimes the rabbits misjudged their run or believed they were far enough away from the tractor and they were harvested along with the grass. The rooks were well aware of this and they had already started to congregate in the tall trees by the side of the field.

Trying not to dwell on this fact, Sandy decided to ask the girls about the remains of the bridge which obviously used to span the canal just in front of Cockshott Bridge.

'That's when we used to have a railway in Barlick,' said Ellen, making it sound as if she remembered when it was, despite the fact that it had obviously been not only derelict, but had had the majority of it missing for probably around fifty years.

'It was built in the late eighteen-hundreds and came pretty much through where the school is now. The last train into Barlick was in the mid sixties, but this bridge had gone long before that.' Esther seemed to be a mine of information and with her last discourse only moments out of her mouth, she was climbing up the side of the bridge.

'Come on,' she shouted, 'last one up doesn't get picked for netball.'

Sandy was up the side like a rat up a drain. Ellen, who obviously had no intention of being on anyone's netball team, climbed sedately up behind them.

From the top you got a great view up and down the canal, and surprisingly there was absolutely nothing to stop you falling off the top. No wall, no fence, nothing. Sandy wondered how, in these days of stupid health and safety rules, the current owner was not being prosecuted for lack of care. Anyway, you got a clear view across Lower Park to the school beyond. When you turned around, you could see where the railway track used to be, although it was now nothing more than a pathway, hedged on either side by brambles and raspberry canes. 'I must remember that for when they get ripe,' thought Sandy.

Boo, being possibly the most sensible one out

of the four, was staying well back from the edge. She seemed to sense danger and understandably had no appetite for it. She preferred to rummage through the bottom of a crisp packet, left by one of the kids who cut through this way to and from school.

There was no sign now of where the bridge had been on the other side of the canal, no structures, no piles of stone and no obvious trackway. Time and farming had erased that part of the railway and buildings like the school had removed the rest. It was likely that the dry stone walls she could see had stones in them from the old bridge and that the trees that ran in a straight line used to run parallel with the railway, but that was just a guess.

The girls scrambled down the bank and on to the towpath, stopping only briefly to make sure that Boo didn't trip over as she came down. Boo, it transpired, did not always have the best sense of balance.

Chapter 4

The day dragged on, due to the promise of netball, and Sandy found herself constantly looking out of the window and daydreaming.

English turned into Maths and then into Geography before the bell went for lunch. Lunches were staggered at the school to minimise the rush on the dining hall and to spread out the lessons and breaks for the different age groups. Sandy looked for Esther and Ellen to ask which team they were trying out for. She imagined it would be the first team, while she was probably going to try for the under 13s. She hoped the trials would be at different times so she could watch and, to be truthful, be watched, because she was looking forward to showing everyone how good she was.

History, double Science and then Music brought

an end to the day. She had studiously avoided being drawn into any discussions with the teachers and had been on her best behaviour in case she had slipped up and ended the day in detention.

She rushed out of the classroom and headed straight for the girls' changing room. There were lots of people putting on their gym kits and Sandy studied her potential competitors as she changed in a corner. There were obviously quite a number of people trying out and she hoped that she was going to be up to the job at hand. Her early confidence began to ebb away as she listened to the chatter of the other girls discussing previous victories and 'awesome' shots that sounded way too good to be real. However, she steeled herself for the job at hand and headed out with the masses.

She kept looking this way and that to see where her friends were, but so far they were a no-show. 'Ah well,' she thought, 'it would have been nice to have some support, but it's not the end of the world.'

'Under 13s, 14s, 15s and under 16s, over here please! Four distinct groups, girls, surely that isn't too complicated for you?'

The crowd split into four groups, although 'distinct' was not quite the word for it. Everyone seemed to be talking and no one seemed to be listening.

'We will have two games going on at the same time,' shouted the teacher, 'one a mixture of 13s and 14s, the other 15s and 16s. Kindly split yourselves up into teams or I will have to do it for you.'

Sandy muscled her way into one group, making sure she was not left out. Bizarrely the numbers seemed to work out well and the two opposing groups headed off towards the courts.

'People on the left grab a bib, people on the right just play in your T-shirts.'

A group of year 11 boys sniggered.

'That would be worth seeing,' quipped a tall, dark-haired boy.

'Shut up, Wood,' bellowed the teacher, 'you know exactly what I meant.'

Netball was always one girls' sport that seemed to attract the boys as spectators. I am fairly sure it was a genuine interest in the sport rather than anything to do with the short skirts!

Miss Simpson stepped forward to take control of their game and quickly explained what was going to happen.

'We will mix things up, changing people and positions today, so the emphasis is on trying to make an impression rather than being on the winning team. Play your hardest, play your best, and we will pick the teams from notes we make during this trial. We will then post the teams and subs on the noticeboard at the end of the week.'

Sandy had always played at Goal Attack previously, and being determined to give herself the best chance to shine, she immediately took up this position on the court, although another girl seemed to have the same idea.

The whistle blew and all hell broke loose. Girls tripped over their own feet, they ran in random directions shouting for the ball, and passes bounced off the backs of other people. Sandy couldn't believe it. She stood in the centre of the court and just shook her head. She had been expecting a level of near professionalism and what she had got was pure chaos.

Miss Simpson blew her whistle again, this time so vigorously that Sandy thought the pea was likely to come out, if indeed whistles had peas any more.

'What the hell was all that about?' bellowed Miss Simpson, barely believing what she had just seen. 'Even those of you who were on the team last year seem completely incapable of running in a straight line, never mind catching the ball. If you can't do any better than that, we might as well just head in now. Last chance,' and she blew the whistle again.

It was a relative transformation. This time the girls stopped talking and started concentrating.

None of them wanted to head back to the changing rooms – after all, they had come out to try to get in the team and that was still what they wanted. Having said that, the operative word here was 'relative'. It was still not pretty by a long way, but at least it didn't look like a collection of complete novices.

The girls ran in all directions, trying to find an unmarked space, but the number of successful passes could be counted on the fingers of one hand. Sandy found herself out on her own and shouted to the centre to pass her the ball. Waving her arms high above her head, she suddenly saw the ball hurtling towards her. Well, not so much towards her as straight past her and well out of reach.

'Sorry,' shouted Sandy, 'couldn't quite reach it.'

She thought that taking this tack was probably better in the long run rather than shouting what she really thought about the pass.

The game started again and the ball went up and down the court from Goal Keeper to Centre, from Centre to Wing Attack from Wing Attack to Goal Shooter and then back. Sandy kept pace and tried her best to ensure she was being seen to be in the right place by Miss Simpson. She was determined to get on the team, but was beginning to get frustrated by the fact that she hardly seemed to be getting her hands anywhere near the ball.

She cut inside her marker and screamed at Charlotte, the Centre, to pass it. Charlotte looked around, trying to decide what to do as she was being severely harassed by the opposition. She launched the ball in an attempt to out-manoeuvre her opponent, but the ball winged its way quietly out of play.

'For God's sake,' blurted Sandy, 'I was open, what the hell was that?'

She had unwittingly mimicked the teacher, hoping that it would have far more of an impact.

Charlotte hung her head but said nothing. The ball was back in play and Sandy regretted her outburst. She was trying to make friends and get in the school team. Outbursts like that were unlikely to help her achieve her goals.

Suddenly she saw her chance and ran quickly in to space.

'In front of me,' she shouted and Charlotte passed the ball over the head of her marking Centre and directly into Sandy's path.

Sandy grabbed at the ball, wanting to make sure this one counted. She slowly and deliberately planted her feet and looked for the Goal Shooter. She was unmarked and Sandy weighed up how hard she should pass. She raised her arms to send the ball on its way and ... 'What the ...?'

Sandy didn't have the ball. In her rush to make

an impression she had obviously missed it completely and as she turned her head, she saw the ball slowly bouncing across the court and being picked up by Wing Attack on the other side.

'I can't believe it,' she thought. 'My one chance to show what I can really do and I blew it.'

She knew that time was running out so she decided to redouble her efforts for the remaining few minutes.

The whistle blew.

'OK,' said Miss Simpson, 'that was far from memorable, but I guess it's as good as it's going to get. The teams and subs will be on the board by the end of the week and I can assure you we are going to have a lot of practising to do before the first game. At the moment you would be an embarrassment to the school. I didn't see a single person out there today who impressed me.'

Sandy was furious. She was furious with her team, she was furious with the opposition and she was furious with herself. She had so wanted to show Miss Simpson what she was capable of.

The girls started to walk off the court to pick up their sweat shirts and hoodies.

Sandy could not contain her anger and frustration any longer. She bent down to pick up a ball that was close by and in an instant it was flying towards the net at the end of the court next to

Miss Simpson. While it seemed to happen so quickly that she didn't even remember throwing the ball, it all seemed to go in slow motion from that point.

One by one the girls looked up to see the ball cutting its way through the air and one by one they went quiet, as did all the spectators.

The ball didn't even touch the rim. It dropped in with a satisfying 'swish' as it hit the netting on the way through.

The girls watching the whole incident were slack-jawed. No one had ever seen anything like it before.

'Who threw that?' asked Miss Simpson finally, breaking the eerie silence.

Sandy raised her hand, a grin playing on her lips.

'Now they will notice me,' she thought.

Sandy could hear a single person clapping slowly but deliberately somewhere off to her left. She turned towards the school, to see Ellen sat on the grass with a big smile on her face.

'Very good,' she shouted, 'excellent.'

Sandy felt a warm glow spreading through her body. She was inwardly delighted that someone, and in particular Ellen, had seen her amazing shot. She began to walk slowly across the court. Halfway across, she turned to wink at the girls who had now congregated under the net and then she turned back to finish her proud strut to where she had left her bag.

'Did you see that last shot?' she asked, knowing full well that Ellen had, otherwise she wouldn't have been clapping.

'Quality,' she said, now standing and clapping in an exaggerated fashion. 'Even Esther would have been impressed.'

'Where is she?' asked Sandy, 'I thought she was going to try out today.'

'No idea. My guess is either she changed her mind because she didn't get picked last year, or she has got into trouble during the day and is in detention somewhere. Could be either.'

Ellen said it in such a matter of fact manner that Sandy guessed this was not an unusual occurrence. She guessed they would catch up with her later, so she went back to giving Ellen a blow-by-blow account of what had happened during the trial, without knowing how long she had been there. Ellen listened politely, chipping in with the odd comment when it seemed appropriate.

They left arm in arm, not bothering to look back again at the court. Had they done so they would have found a huge gaggle of girls surrounding the gym teacher, all talking and no one listening, each one wanting to tell the others, who obviously already knew, that they had just witnessed the most incredible sight they had ever seen.

By the time they had wandered down across the field and joined the marina road, Sandy realised that all they had talked about was her and the netball trial.

'How was your day?' she asked, hoping that Ellen hadn't got bored with the whole conversation.

'Quiet,' she said, 'but that's how I like it, to be honest.'

Sandy remembered a saying that someone had told her a long time ago. 'When there is nothing to be said, some fool always says it.'

Taking the advice previously given her, she shut up and was content to walk back along the canal bank in relative silence, just enjoying the fact that she had someone to walk with and basking in the cooling rays of the late summer sun.

Chapter 5

As they approached the narrowboat, Sandy noticed a jogger in the distance. She recognised the outline of Val coming towards them and she turned and told Ellen about her and her son in the buggy.

Val saw Sandy and slowed down to a complete stop by the side of the boat. She took out her ear pieces and turned and said hello to Sandy.

'Hi,' she replied, 'this is my friend Ellen who lives on this boat.'

Val turned to speak to Ellen, but she wasn't there. She was already down on her knees smiling at the ever-grinning Matthew in the buggy.

Val smiled. 'That's ...'

'Matthew,' said Ellen, 'Sandy has already told me what a cute little bundle of joy he is.'

Sandy didn't remember ever having said that, but seeing the proud look on Val's face she decided to say nothing. Everyone loves being told their kids are cute.

'Have you lived on the boat long?' asked Val, truly interested, as she had never met anyone who had lived on a boat before.

'Sometimes it seems like forever,' laughed Ellen.

'Doesn't it get cold?'

'Well, in the winter it can get a bit nippy, but we have a log-burning stove which keeps us pretty warm and to be honest, the cold doesn't really bother me that much. During the summer it can actually get too hot, a bit like living in a tin can, but you can always open windows. You see, the canal doesn't go to the same extremes as the air. Being water, it tends to hold a more steady temperature and so it kind of acts like a heat exchanger.'

Val and Sandy both looked impressed. Neither had really thought about that before, never really had a need to. Seemed to make sense though.

'Well,' said Val, 'it was a pleasure to meet you and I am sure we will see each other again – I run along here all the time.'

With that, she plugged her ears back in and switched on her music.

Just then there was a movement in the galley. Ellen and Sandy both waved and the man looked up. Val waved too, and the man raised his hand to reciprocate with a smile.

'Bye, Matthew,' they both shouted as Val headed off down the towpath with the buggy in front. A little hand came out of the side to show he had heard and then they were gone.

'Up here!' came a voice and the girls looked to see Esther on the bridge. 'You have to see this.'

'I wonder what she has found now?' asked Ellen, almost not wanting to know the answer, based on previous experiences. Often the things that Esther found were not that palatable; a dead badger, a duck floating down the canal, its body distended with the gases given off by its rotting stomach, or a wasps' nest dangerously full of wasps. On other occasions it would be a rare orchid growing in the long grass or a nest of baby field mice. You could just never be sure with Esther.

'Come on,' she shouted and Sandy and Ellen ran along the path to catch her.

As they got closer, Esther disappeared from view. She had ducked down under the bridge and so the girls followed suit. When they came out of the other side, they saw Esther disappearing over the dry stone wall behind the Anchor. She waved to make sure they had seen her and then she was gone from view again.

Sandy and Ellen followed, looking over their

shoulders to make sure that no one was watching them. They felt sure they shouldn't be there and the last thing they wanted was to get caught.

Esther was kneeling down by a small window that was set in the wall just above ground level. She lifted the window open and turned to smile at the others.

'Fancy an adventure?'

While they knew they shouldn't, Sandy and Ellen were both up for whatever trouble it was that Esther was about to get them in to. The three of them slid through the window and down on to a dark set of steps. They gently let the window shut behind them, much to the consternation of Boo who had been left outside. All she could do now was watch them through the dirty pane of glass, which was virtually impossible as they were now in a dark cellar.

All around them were wires and pipes that were hung from the walls and a gentle hum of electric motors filled the still air. A stale smell of beer pervaded the atmosphere, mixing gently with a musty smell of history.

The building dated back to 1655 and was built on the old Pack Horse Way, a road used by drovers and salters, people bringing salt from Cheshire to Yorkshire. That is where the name of the village Salterforth came from. During the excavation of the canal from 1770 to 1816, the original hostelry, called the Traveller's Rest, was replaced by a new building, The Canal Tavern, which was built on top of it, because of the rise in the water level. This was later renamed The Anchor Inn at the turn of the century. Not surprising that there was a damp feel to the cellar, being so close to the canal.

'This way,' whispered Esther as she quietly descended the cellar stairs.

The girls followed, feeling their way down the wall, attempting to steady themselves as they stepped in to the darkness.

Suddenly a light came on. Sandy gasped, wondering just how much trouble she was going to be in now that they had been discovered trespassing. She knew that whatever was about to happen would be nothing compared with the reaction that she was going to get when she got home.

'That's better,' said Esther, 'at least we can see now that I've put the light on.'

Ellen slapped Esther across the back of the head.

'What was that for?'

'You scared the crap out of us, that's what for.'

Sandy let out a sigh of relief. That was way too close for her liking. She hated getting in trouble or having people feeling disappointed with her.

Esther pushed open a door and made a

triumphant noise as if she had just got to the end of a magic trick. 'Ta dah!' and she held out a hand towards the room.

'Wow!' That was all that Sandy could say

In front of her was a veritable Aladdin's Cave. Hanging from the ceiling were hundreds of needle-thin stalactites, making the place look like an ice grotto. Below them were stalagmites pushing up from the floor like seedlings desperately trying to find light. The whole thing was magical.

The glow from the light bulb bounced off the needles, which were covered by a thin sheen of dampness. The small ridges scattered the light in all directions and eerie shadows were cast against the walls and floor.

Esther moved from side to side, dancing slowly, waving her arms in time to some silent music playing in her head. Her shadow was cut into vertical sections like a boiled egg being passed through a slicer. Slowly she moved forward towards the needles.

'Don't!' shouted Ellen. 'If you break them we will get into so much trouble.'

Esther took no notice and slid slowly in between the hanging stems.

Sandy held her breath. She couldn't see how she was doing it, but somehow Esther was carefully making her way to the back of the room. A single touch would bring the needles crashing down, but somehow she squirmed her way through without touching a thing. The only problem was that she now had to get back again without upsetting anything.

Suddenly there was a noise from behind the door at the top of the stairs. Sandy looked at Ellen, panic written all across her face.

'Quick, hide!' whispered Ellen as she flicked the switch off.

They ducked down behind a wall of empty barrels that had been set aside at the bottom of the stairs and hoped they wouldn't be seen.

The light was turned on again and a mountain of a man descended the stairs. He was humming to himself as he came ever closer to the girls, step by step. He stopped. They couldn't see what he was doing or why he had stopped so suddenly. They were keeping their heads down and praying. He walked across to the stalactite room and gazed inside. The humming ceased. The girls held their breath, they were moments away from discovery. Esther could see his silhouette as she stood stock still in the semi darkness. He was framed by the door jamb and backlit by the bulb in the cellar. He looked huge and menacing and she waited for the explosion which was bound to come.

She was used to being in scrapes, it had seemed

like a way of life to her. She remembered the aftermath of when she had released the moorings on the boat next to hers one evening when she was only about seven. No one had noticed until a barge heading along the canal had collided with it and knocked the occupants off their seats while having dinner. She had escaped punishment because she had never admitted to it.

She remembered the bag of flour she had tipped off the Kelbrook Bridge some years earlier, covering not one, but two narrowboats and their owners in a fine cloud of white powder. Again, she had escaped any retribution because she had turned and bolted across the fields and up Hurst Hill towards Letcliffe Park.

She even remembered the time she had let all of the frogs out of their jars in Biology because she was sure they were going to be asked to dissect them. It turns out that they were just supposed to study the way they jumped. As it happened they all managed to do that very well as they tried to retrieve 20 lively animals from the classroom floor.

It is amazing just how much you can remember in a split second when you think your life is going to end. 'Guess this is what they mean by your life flashing before you,' she thought to herself as she closed her eyes and wished herself invisible.

The humming started again, just as abruptly as

it had stopped. Although they still couldn't see him, by virtue of their heads being buried against the floor, the girls heard him close the door. Silently the barman wondered why it was open in the first place, but his head was filled with more important things, like not forgetting the order of the man upstairs that had initiated his trip to the cellar and making sure that he put the right barrel on the right pipe. Only last week he had mistakenly tapped a firkin of John Smiths with the pipe from the Copper Dragon pump and the locals were never going to let him live that one down. He turned on his heels and grabbed one of the barrels, in fact the barrel that was right in front of Ellen. He obviously wasn't concentrating as he swung it up on to his shoulder and span around without noticing the exposed body of the cowering girl. He marched across to the other side of the cellar and they heard the distinctive sound of gas escaping as he released the empty keg and then replaced it with the new one. With a spring in his step he started up the stairs, taking two at a time, and switched the light off again when he reached the top. All three girls let out a joint sigh of relief.

The door to the stalactite room gingerly swung open, its hinges creaking in the darkness. The only light now was the delicate shaft emanating from the window that they had used to enter the cellar.

It lit up the door like a dull spotlight focused on the main character on a theatre stage.

Esther's face appeared, a huge grin spreading across from ear to ear.

'Anyone want to get out of here?'

No one needed a second invitation.

Back up the stairs, out through the window and then over the wall. All done surgically and precisely without a single second wasted and with such speed that I swear not a single foot touched the ground. Once they were all on the bank they collapsed in a heap and burst out laughing. It started out as a release of nervous tension, but then it quickly progressed to a deep raucous belly laugh, as they lay on their backs, looking up at the sky and thanking their lucky stars that they hadn't been apprehended.

Boo took this as an invitation to join in and leapt upon the first body she could reach. This was one of those moments that would be remembered well into adulthood. We can all recall such moments from our youth when the world seemed nothing more than a simple play thing, where nothing truly mattered except the next adventure.

They tumbled around on the grass by the water; legs, arms, tails – OK, only one tail – and peals of laughter intermixed with the excited barking of the terrier. Life, it has to be said, was good.

Chapter 6

The remainder of the week was spent keeping their heads down at school, making the most of their free time along the towpath and, for Sandy at least, waiting to read the team sheet.

Friday came and she could hardly contain her enthusiasm. She managed to control the urge to run to school, primarily because she knew there would be no point in getting there before it opened, before the staff arrived and before the posting went up, but it was still a strong urge nevertheless.

She found herself waiting by her 'personal fountain of life's precious elixir,' desperately awaiting the appearance of her friends from the boat. After what seemed like hours, but was in reality only about six minutes, the pair came barrelling off the boat in their usual style, closely followed by a manic Boo.

She ran up to great them both with a hug. Today was going to be a good day.

They stopped briefly to wave goodbye through the window, by now a morning ritual, and then chatted all the way to the marina road about this and that, but the conversations always returned to netball. Sandy knew what position she wanted and she was worried that she might not get it. That said, just being in the team would be wonderful and then she could always change position after she had shown her stuff in the first proper game.

The lists were to be posted by first break, which obviously meant the first lessons of the day just dragged by. Sandy was quite sure that she could see the second hand of the clock in her form room going backwards. She knew you could buy clocks like that, but couldn't believe the school would have done so.

Who knew that quadratic equations could be so boring? OK, bad example, everybody knew they were boring, even the mathematicians who used them, but this was a whole new level of boring. This was the sort of boring that made you want to stick drawing pins into your own eyes just to break the monotony!

Praise the Lord, Maths had finished and now all she had to do was survive English Lit; be still my beating heart, today was going to be Poetry.

I wander'd lonely as a cloud
That floats on high o'er vales and hills
When all at once I saw a crowd
A host, of golden daffodils
Beside the lake, beneath the trees
Fluttering and dancing in the breeze.

'Who knows who wrote these immortal words?' asked Mr Strathmore, the English Lit teacher.

Silence echoed around the classroom.

'Come on,' thought Sandy, 'everyone knows that one, surely?'

She kept quiet and the noise of feet shuffling and pens tapping on desks was deafening.

'One of the greatest poets in English history.'

Still no answer.

'Has a visitors' centre in Grasmere, in the Lake District.'

'You have to admire Mr Strathmore's tenacity' thought Sandy

'Born in 1770.'

He might as well have been from another planet. The faces in the classroom couldn't have been any blanker if he had been speaking Swahili.

'Contemporary of Samuel Taylor Coleridge.'

More nothing.

'Give me a break here, people. Surely someone

has heard of him.'

'Wordsworth,' said Sandy quietly. She recognised the poem and somewhere deep in her memory a thought had stirred.

'I'm sorry, did someone say something?'

'Wordsworth,' she repeated, this time in a more confident manner.

'Anybody?' pleaded Strathmore.

'Wordsworth!' bellowed Sandy.

'Wordsworth. William Wordsworth, born 1770, died 1850. Sometimes I despair. Let's try another one.

> *Sometimes I just feel like, quittin'*
> *I still might*
> *Why do I put up this fight*
> *Why do I still write*
> *Sometimes it's hard enough*
> *Just dealin' with real life*
> *Sometimes I wanna jump on stage*
> *And just kill mics*
> *And show these people*
> *What my level of skill's like*
> *But I'm still white*
> *Sometimes I just hate life*
> *Somethin ain't right*
> *Hit the brake lights*
> *Case of the stage fright*

Drawin' a blank like.

Any takers?'

About half the class thrust their hands in to the air, but Sandy looked bemused.

'Eminem' they shouted en masse, looking very pleased with themselves.

'I knew that too,' thought Sandy.

'So, you are not complete halfwits then,' stated Mr Strathmore. 'Just lacking a little in the classics. I want you all to read "I wandered lonely as a cloud" and write me two sides of A4 as a critique. For those of you who don't know what a critique is, Google it, but don't just cut and paste from the internet because I've seen most of them before and will offer up a detention as a prize to anyone stupid enough to do it.'

And with that, the bell went for break.

Sandy raced down the corridor to look at the games notice board. Nothing. She couldn't believe it. More girls started appearing, each one just as eager to see if they had made the team.

Eventually Miss Simpson arrived.

'Make way,' she said, pushing her way through the jostling throng.

'If you haven't made it on to the list, please still come to practise, as we will be switching players out, if you can show we have made a mistake. We will also be giving people a chance to demonstrate willingness and enthusiasm, something that is sadly lacking with some members of the team, and you know who you are.'

With that she left, heading back to a cup of coffee already poured in the staff room.

The girls pushed and shoved to see the list. Sandy managed to position herself to get a good look. Not there on the first team, but then again she hadn't really expected it to be. She was new, there were a lot of older girls and she was quite sure that once she had established herself, she would soon move up the ranks. Not on the second team either. In fact, as she looked, her name didn't appear on any of the team sheets, either as a player or a sub. Her heart sank. She checked again and rechecked to make sure she hadn't made a mistake. Nothing. It was like a kick in the teeth.

Gradually the others girls drifted away in twos and threes leaving Sandy as a sad single outline against the freshly painted wall. She couldn't believe it. How could they have left her out? If they thought that she was going to still come to practises, they could forget it. Now she understood why she hadn't seen Esther at the trial. If she had been treated like this the year before, Sandy completely understood why she hadn't bothered to show up this year.

Five minutes later Sandy was crossing the field

towards the marina. She glanced to the right and through the spindly willow hedge to see a man on his red tractor mower cutting the grass. For a moment she wished she was him, apparently without a care in the world, apart from trying to get the stripes in the lawn right. She knew she was going to get into terrible trouble for playing truant, but at this moment she didn't care.

She passed a group of first years who were surreptitiously puffing on cigarettes, obviously having decided that bunking off alone wasn't good enough and that they might as well compound the offence by smoking, to boot. She paid them no heed and just strode past, eyes firmly glued on the floor, quietly still seething inside.

She crossed the bridge and instead of turning along the canal, she continued straight ahead, through the gates and into the farmer's fields opposite. The cows looked at her in that interested way that only cows know how to look, half terrified and half inquisitive, and then they returned to the important job of chewing grass. She stopped briefly to look at the herd of deer that was up on the hill and tried to spot the llama that lived in among the sheep, but then continued along parallel to the stone wall. She came to a halt before the next gate and then using one of the lower stones as a step, reached up to lean over the wall to look at, of all things, the family of wallabies that lived in a green plastic drum. 'Bizarre,' she thought, that Barlick had wallabies, but really didn't think any more about it than that. They had been there for years and people had got used to them, at least those that knew they were there. They were easily missed, being just far enough off the towpath not to be seen.

They looked at each other for a couple of minutes, neither very interested in the other, and then she moved on. Up the path to the brow of the hill, where she turned and admired the panoramic view down over the marina and further, up to the school, where she knew she should be, but had no qualms about not being. How could they leave her out? She would show them! Deep down she knew that skipping school was going to do nothing more than get her in trouble, both back at school and at home, but at this moment, logic and common sense had nothing to do with her decisions. These were purely emotionally driven.

When she reached the kissing gate at Ben Lane she took one last look across the valley and turned her back on education for the rest of the day. There were better things to do, places to explore, new things to see.

She turned left and walked the twenty or thirty metres to the old crossroads of the foot paths and took the path on her right hand side by the entrance to Kayfields. She cut across the pasture, keeping tight to the right as the cows had turned most of the ground into a sea of mud. Soon the farm came into sight and she thought she had better keep going in case they saw her and reported her as AWOL. In reality it was so unlikely. Kids skived off school so often these days and the general apathy of people was amazing. Add that to the fact that the old adage of 'no good deed goes unpunished' seemed to be true, meaning most folk these days kept themselves to themselves. There were too many cases of good Samaritans getting into trouble with the law for stepping in to help strangers or reporting misdeeds and, for that matter, too many kids and parents taking action against teachers for what used to be considered good discipline. However, none of that made any difference to Sandy at that moment. She just wanted to get past the farm and into more open countryside.

She tiptoed across the turf that had been cut up by the regular to-ings and fro-ings of the dairy herd, trying to keep on the high points so as not to get sucked down in to the mire. Across the farm track and through the gate and now she had the farm behind her. Two horses wandered across to see what she was up to and Sandy waited patiently for them to make their way across to her. They flicked their tails from side to side to try and disperse the flies that were permanently buzzing around their bodies. She ran her hand along their muzzles and watched them as they playfully tried to push each other out of the way. She marvelled at how they could lean so heavily on the barbed wire fence without hurting themselves. She could see the points pushing against their skin, but it looked more likely that the fence posts would give way before any puncture occurred.

It is always remarkably therapeutic stroking animals and Sandy began to feel her anger ebbing away. She looked deep into their eyes and ran her hands through their manes. It was as if there was a connection, but no sooner had she thought this than they turned and galloped off to the other side of the field.

This did nothing to improve her mood, so she turned and continued along the path keeping close to the hedge, as this made her less obvious. As she reached the corner of the field, the path opened out on to Ghyll Lane. She remembered having come this way early in the summer, just after moving to Salterforth, when she was in exploration mode. She couldn't remember where it came out, but that wasn't going to stop her. She strode purposefully down the lane ensuring that she was putting further distance between her and school.

As the lane took a sharp left, Sandy stood

looking at the beautiful old building of St Mary-le-Gill Church. Founded in the 12th century, alterations and time had ensured that very little remained of its original structure. The Ley Brothers that helped build Fountains Abbey had been responsible for this church. They had started once before, but then had to abandon their efforts due to poor harvests and continual thievery. They had, however, returned some ten years later and second time around had done an excellent job, but sadly now only a couple of windows were thought to be original, along with a stone coffin that lay alongside the porch.

Sandy walked up to the front of the church and despite it having steel rail outer and solid wood inner doors, she found the access surprisingly easy. She made her way past the huge font stone and down through the rows of pews before taking a seat at the front. The church was totally dominated by an impressive three-tiered pulpit, the likes of which Sandy had never seen before.

She let her head flop backwards and she marvelled at the wooden beams that criss-crossed the roof space and had done so for nearly 700 years since its first roof renovation.

'If only they could talk,' she said out loud, 'what tales they could tell.'

'You OK?'

Sandy jumped and her head snapped forward nearly giving her whiplash.

'How long have you been there?' she asked, turning to face Ellen.

'I followed you in. In fact I've been following you ever since I saw your face in the corridor by the games board. I saw your name wasn't there and waited until you arrived to find out for yourself. Since then I've been shadowing you across the fields. Thought you might want someone to talk to.'

Sandy didn't know what to say. This was the first time she had ever had a friend that cared this much. In fact, this was probably the first time she could remember that she actually had a friend, full stop.

'Esther was exactly the same last year, so I kind of expected a similar reaction from you.'

Sandy felt a little better, knowing that she hadn't been alone feeling like this. Now she definitely understood why Esther hadn't been at the trial. It really sucked.

'What you need,' said Ellen 'is something to take your mind off things. Follow me.'

Sandy had no idea what she had planned, but she didn't really care. Anyone who was prepared to miss school to make sure you were OK was good enough for her. Whatever she had in mind was just great by Sandy.

Ellen led her out of the church and through the graveyard. It had to be said, it was a pretty graveyard, if indeed you could have such a thing, but it did seem a little strange having a public footpath wending its way through the graves. As they walked, Sandy looked at the various headstones, amazed at how old some of them were. There were statuesque marble uprights and others that looked like picnic tables. Sandy wondered if the bodies were really still there underneath the tablets, well at the least the skeletons. She kept searching to try and find the oldest date that was still legible, while not falling too far behind Ellen. John Monckes, 1664, was the best she could find under the circumstances and rather than being over a grave, this headstone was now part of the pathway leading to the church.

After a brief walk, they left the graveyard behind them and cut down the path by the side of the golf club, coming out on to Skipton Road, opposite the Rolls Royce complex. Sandy had never been here before, but she knew she couldn't be far from her beloved canal.

They crossed over the road and headed off down Greenberfield Lane, stopping when they reached the bridge.

'Look,' said Ellen, pointing up towards the lock keeper's cottage, 'there's Esther.'

Chapter 7

Sandy looked up and saw her. She was sitting cross-legged on top of their narrowboat, which was just about to enter the lock, Boo loyally tucked in by her side.

Ellen smiled when she saw the look on Sandy's face. She had lit up and the disappointment of the netball was quickly forgotten.

'He decided to take the boat out to blow the cobwebs off the engine. Fancy a trip along the canal?'

Sandy had never actually been anywhere on a boat before. Sure she had been aboard this one while it was moored up, but not when it had been moving.

'Come on,' shouted Ellen as she started running towards the lock, 'last one on board pumps the bilge.'

Sandy had no idea what this meant but she assumed it wouldn't be good or it wouldn't have been a forfeit. She sprinted past Ellen and headed up the towpath towards the boat. By now Esther was waving to the pair of them and Boo was barking madly.

'Forget the team, forget Miss Simpson and forget school. We are Marton bound!' she screamed as Sandy clambered on board.

'Guess you've got to plump the bulge,' said Sandy looking back at Ellen over her shoulder, trying to fit in.

'Close enough,' giggled Ellen. Esther just looked bemused.

'This lock is the highest point on the Leeds and Liverpool canal,' said Esther. 'It's 149 metres above the sea and runs at this height all the way through the Foulridge Tunnel to near Barrowford, where the next lock is. Limestone and coal used to travel from one side of the country to the other and when the old boatmen reached this stretch, they knew they were on the downward run.'

Sandy never ceased to be amazed at the complexity of Esther. One minute she was fishing frogs out of the canal, the next she was espousing about the history of the industrial revolution and with some confidence. Coming from someone else, it would probably have been incredibly boring, but as it was, Sandy found it fascinating and it actually sank in.

The three girls, four including Boo, were now all sitting quietly on the top of the roof, waiting to pass into the lock.

Nick was at the helm, but at the moment they were not going anywhere, as the mooring ropes were still holding them fast to the bank. He was waiting for the Dutch Barge coming through the lock in the opposite direction to clear before being able to steer *Rag Albert* through the top gate. The water was already rushing in and the barge was slowly rising to meet the same level as the girls and their narrowboat. Nick could see they were getting close, so he began to make ready.

'All hands on deck and belay the bow rope!' he shouted.

'What did he say?' asked Sandy, not really sure what was going on.

'Oh, don't worry about him, just sit back and enjoy the ride,' said Ellen, lying back and looking for shapes in the clouds.

Nick chuckled; he had had the same routine since before his wife had died. During the last months of her life she had not been strong enough to help out with the physical side of boating, but he still called out the directions and then did them all himself. She would sit on deck, when the weather was good enough, and smile as he went about his business. Now he continued to call out the same commands in the same way, whether there was anyone else on the boat or not. It was his way of keeping her with him.

'Do we need to do anything?' asked Sandy, watching Nick making his way down the bank.

'Nah, he loves being in charge and doing everything himself.'

It certainly did look that way. Nick had the diesel engine ticking over and was merrily releasing the bow rope holding the boat near the bank. He rolled the painter lovingly into a beautifully symmetrical circle which he then laid on the deck before gently pushing the boat away from the bank.

He walked back up the path towards the stern which was now the only place that the boat was tethered. Looking back towards the lock he saw that the barge master was now opening the upstream gate. He had his back braced against the huge square wooden swing beam and was pushing his thick soled boots against the ground, slowly walking backwards.

Taking this as his signal, Nick shouted 'Release the stern' and then smiled as he did just that himself.

Esther and Ellen just shook their heads.

'He doesn't get any better with age!'

Nick jumped back on to the boat and grabbed the tiller, making sure that he was going to steer well away from the traffic that was now making its way out of the lock.

With a simple nod of the head towards each other, so subtle that it would probably have been missed by those not associated with the water, the two 'Captains' acknowledged each other's craft and skill and then, as the old saying goes, they became ships that passed in the night, except of course it was not even the middle of the day yet.

Nick steered his boat into the space left by the exiting barge. The whole of the pressure of the canal was now pushing against the downstream gate which was angled in towards the lock, using the weight of the water to seal it shut. Once inside and after having taken a turn of the top line around the bollard, Nick jumped back off the boat, windlass in hands and walked back to swing the gates shut behind them. Once he was comfortable that things were as they should be, he slowly opened the sluice to let the water out. Using the line, he controlled the movement of the boat during the descent, keeping it as far forward as possible so as not to let the rudder collide with the upper gate.

Sandy was surprised – and slightly scared if the truth be known – by the noise made by the water streaming out of the lock. The boat began to drop, unnervingly making it look as if the towpath was moving upwards, and slowly the stone-built insides of the lock became exposed.

Nick kept a very close eye on *Rag Albert* as the boat gradually dropped, bobbing in the water like a cork, albeit a very large cork.

Sandy was looking this way and that, soaking up every moment of this new experience.

'See, it's an elephant,' explained Ellen, 'trunk top left and legs down to the right.'

'I see what you mean,' replied Esther, 'but it looks more like a panda if you hold your head slightly to the left.'

Sandy looked around to see that they were both now lying on their backs looking up at the clouds. They had obviously been through locks so many times that the excitement had now gone out of it. It wasn't so much being blasé, more just an expression of a comfortable routine brought on by experience.

As the levels evened out, the noise started to fade from a rushing to a gentle bubbling. Nick had controlled the boat well and although it had bobbed around a little, it had barely touched the side. He swiftly opened the gates and then bowhauled the boat forward to ensure they didn't swing close on them. Holding the rope over his arm, he climbed carefully down the ladder, making sure that he didn't slip, as that would be disastrous. Once at boat height he stepped on to the gunwales and made his way back to the stern. Apart from being safer than walking along the roof, this also meant that the girls didn't need to move and risk Boo slipping over the side. While she was used to living on the boat she was, when all's said and done, still a dog.

Nick engaged the engine and they started to make their way out, taking care not to buffet the boat with the wooden gates. He slowly steered *Rag Albert* to the mooring ring, so that he could tie the boat off and go back and close the lock gates.

As they approached the bank, Sandy jumped up, feeling that she should help in some way, despite being told to just sit back and relax. She slid off the roof on to the bow and went to pick up the mooring line. She seemed to be all fingers and thumbs, surprised at how difficult it was compared to the ease with which Nick had managed it.

'Just leave it,' called Ellen, but Sandy was determined.

The more she tried the more she seemed to be getting nowhere. The more she got nowhere, the more annoyed she got. Just as she was about to lose it, the rope was through the ring and attached with a superb round turn and two half hitches.

'Nice job,' commented Esther, 'couldn't have

done any better myself.'

Proudly, Sandy made her way back up to sit with the girls. She wasn't quite sure how she had managed so well, but she wasn't going to let on.

'Make fast the bow!' shouted Nick, having gently steered the boat into the bank. He had been stuck at the stern and hadn't seen that the bow was already tied up. He sprung on to the towpath and made his way fore.

'What the ...?'

Nick looked at the mooring and then up and down the towpath in an exaggerated manner.

'How on earth did that get tied up?' he said loudly looking back at the boat.

'Oh, don't take any notice of him,' said Ellen. 'He's always making smart-arsed comments like that because he's forever saying he has to do every-thing himself. If I were you I wouldn't bother again.'

Scratching his head Nick walked back, tied off the stern and then went to swing the lower gates shut.

Upon his return he went through his normal routine of shouting out commands and then performing them himself. As he released the bow rope he appeared to smile to himself. Sandy noticed and a grin spread across her lips as she knew he had appreciated her efforts.

Back on board, the engine throbbed into life,

stirring up the water with a mixture of bubbles and river weed and *Rag Albert* headed slowly off towards Marton. The whole lock manoeuvre had taken some twenty minutes and brought home to Sandy the difference in the pace of life on the canal. There was no way to move a boat through any quicker; it took the time it took and that was that. The motors made it easier than back when all the barges were horse drawn, but it was still not a fast pace.

No sooner had they cleared the lock than they were up against another. In fact there were three that came in quick succession. This time, however, Sandy just stayed put and allowed Nick to go through his pre-programmed paces for the last two. He had his routine, it was the same as it had been when he was married and nothing was ever going to change it. Sandy felt like she had intruded with her attempt to help at the top lock, so she vowed to let him carry on in his own sweet way.

The narrowboat engine chugged merrily to itself. Sandy liked the word 'chugged'; it was one of those wonderful onomatopoeic words, like 'cuckoo' or 'whoosh'.

They could all relax now and just enjoy the journey, at least until the next lock. The sun was showering them with golden rays and with the girls lying back on the warm metal roof, it was all they could do to stay awake.

The clouds, few as they now were, hung in the sky like wisps of candyfloss, their edges slowly disappearing before their eyes. The only wind was that generated by the boat forcing its way through the otherwise still air that floated above the canal.

Sandy noticed sounds that she would not normally have noticed. It is amazing how you tune into totally different things when you put yourself in a new situation. Sure, she had been on the canal many times, but always on the towpath and always when she was walking. This was different. There was an underlying thwack, thwack, thwack of the water hitting the hull that supplied the rhythm of the music. The harsh clatter of the wings of battling dragonflies brought in the percussion and the melody came from the numerous birds adorning the undergrowth and bushes. Warblers did exactly what it says on the packet and the dunnocks, chaffinches and thrushes all joined in to produce the soundtrack of the canal.

Sandy lapped up the ambience. It wasn't just the sounds; it was the colours as well. The jade green of the vegetation, the metallic cyans and reds of the damselflies darting to and fro in the reeds and the crystal blue sharpness of the sky. The sheep stood out against the fields like fluffy marshmallows and the ducks scattered in the wake of the boat like flotsam tossed around on the sea. There was just one word to sum it up: magical.

She now understood why people took holidays on narrowboats and she understood why Nick and the girls lived full time on the water.

'Have you guys always lived on *Rag Albert*?' asked Sandy, wondering if they had been born aboard the boat or if they had moved on from a normal house.

'Hatched afloat and will probably die afloat,' explained Esther, who was stripping the leaves off a small branch that she had apparently grabbed when Nick had steered the boat under an overhanging willow on the way to Greenberfield, so as to avoid a novice coming the other way.

'Keep right,' was the rule and don't exceed 4 miles per hour on the canal. It was only a fast walking pace, but seemed sufficient unless you were in an almighty rush. Let's be fair, if you were in an almighty rush you shouldn't be on a boat in the first place.

'Mum died soon after I was born. She loved the whole way of life that came with the canal. 'Enjoy the simple pleasures' dad said she always used to say, 'you never know what the future holds.' Quite prophetic when you look back on it.'

Sandy didn't know what to say. She felt like she was intruding, but Esther seemed so natural in telling her story.

'Dad brought us up on his own. He made a living writing articles for boating magazines and books about the canals. It wasn't a fortune, but it allowed us to live on the boat and not worry where the next meal was coming from.'

'I'm sorry about your mum,' said Sandy, her words carrying the real sadness that she felt about what had happened. 'It must be a great relief to have someone like Nick around to look after you.' She knew relief wasn't the right word, but it is hard to come up with exactly what you want to say when you are halfway through saying it.

'It is. I don't know what we would do without him. He's a bit set in his ways and likes to do it all himself, but we couldn't have anyone better.'

The girls smiled at one another, it was the deepest conversation they had had so far and it brought them closer together. The ensuing silence gave each of them the chance to reflect on what they had and how petty the concerns about not making the netball team seemed now in the grand scheme of things. Sandy felt almost embarrassed about her earlier outburst, but she knew she didn't have to explain or apologise.

Best friends are made through smiles and tears they say – whoever 'they' are.

Chapter 8

Even though time seemed to move slower on the waterways, it was already afternoon and *Rag Albert* was making its way past the back of the Rolls-Royce buildings. The sun glinted off the myriad steel pipes and chimneys making what was predominantly an ugly structure seem almost beautiful, in a purely industrial way, you understand.

Once beyond this point, the canal opened up in to classic English countryside. The rolling green fields were sewn together like a patchwork quilt with dry stone walls providing the stitching. Here and there, the fields were punctuated by old buildings, some in a state of complete disrepair and others having been restored to their former glory. Every now and then, one would appear off in the distance which had been converted into a family dwelling. They made fantastic homes and maintained the beautiful harmony of a bygone era by not changing the external features. They blended into the landscape and preserved a little slice of history, while providing all the necessary mod cons for comfortable living in the twenty-first century.

The canal margins provided the same unspoilt natural habitat as did, surprisingly, the banks of the motorways up and down the UK. Bizarrely, because no one walks along these race tracks, mammals and birds thrive, which is why you often see kestrels hunting alongside the M1. The canal banks, although they see many dog walkers, cyclists and joggers, are relatively untouched, compared with the surrounding fields which are heavily farmed. Therefore, there is a natural concentration of wildlife, although you have to look for it as it prefers not to be on view.

Rag Albert continued its gentle passage, accompanied by the rhythmic throbbing of the engine. It was as if someone was trying to impose the beat of a metronome on to the soundtrack of nature. A nice idea, but unlikely ever to reach the charts.

Soon the travelling band was carefully navigating its way under the bridge at West Marton. The fisherman sitting quietly on the bank waved at them as they rounded the corner under the bridge, probably assuming they had thoughtfully slowed down so as not to interfere with his float. Truth was, it was necessary to slow down or they wouldn't make it through without colliding with the bank. The girls waved back enthusiastically and Boo joined in with a chorus of barks, just as likely to upset the fishing as the sound of the engine. Nick, however, gave a seasoned nod in the direction of the angler, thoughtfully keeping the revs down until he was well clear of the scene.

What little there was of West Marton gave way to more fields and stone walls. The best part of the afternoon was now behind them and the shadows were beginning to lengthen as the sun started to sink slowly in the sky. Sandy had no idea how far they were actually going or when they would be back – and frankly she didn't care. Not a word had been said by any of them for over thirty minutes, but it didn't seem to matter. Everyone was comfortable and Nick looked relaxed and at ease leaning on the tiller, looking every inch the part of a boat Captain.

They had travelled under a number of low stone bridges that afternoon and each time the girls had raised their hands to see if they could touch the underside of the arch. So far only once had they managed, with a stretch, and then they wished they hadn't as years of accumulated spiders' webs, dirt and general grot had been prized off the rendering and had come tumbling down upon them, eliciting shrieks of laughter.

'Ah, here comes the old double bridge,' said Nick, breaking the silence and causing the girls to sit up and take notice.

They were approaching East Marton and in front of them was a rare sight indeed. Where the A59 crosses the canal, there stands a rare double-arched bridge. The original bridge formed the lower arch and then, built upon it so as to allow the engineers to raise the level of the road and eliminate a vicious dip, was a second arch, in keeping with the first but obviously newer.

'Very impressive,' thought Sandy as she felt the engine throttling down as they came nearer, Nick obviously anticipating the narrowing of the canal to almost single file at this point. Glancing to her right, Sandy saw someone leaning up against the bridge so, as she had done all afternoon, she waved, not expecting any reaction. After all, not a single person had bothered to return her wave since they passed the fisherman. This time, however, the man looked up and waved back, slowly at first and then ever more frantically. He seemed excited or nervous – difficult to tell which, really – and now it was difficult to see him anymore as the boat made its way under the bridge.

'Did you see him?' Sandy said, looking over at the two girls.

'See who?' asked Ellen.

'There was a guy on the towpath over there.' Sandy pointed towards where she had just seen him. 'He seemed upset. Come to think of it, not only that, but he was dressed kind of funny as well.'

'Funny ha ha, or funny peculiar?' asked Esther in a not-too-helpful way. 'I mean, was he wearing a clown suit?'

'Shut up!' snapped Ellen. 'What do you mean, Sandy?'

Just as Sandy began to open her mouth, there was a terrible silence that seemed to echo through the cutting. It seems strange to say that silence can do anything like that, but when you have been listening to the plodding throb of a diesel engine all afternoon, its absence is just as noticeable as the noise it makes when it first kicks in.

'What's up?' Esther shouted back to where Nick was looking bemused and turning and returning the ignition key. Nothing. The boat had not stopped, because you cannot just stop a narrowboat when it is underway. The inertia keeps you going and Nick suddenly realised he had taken his eye off the steering once the engine had cut out. He quickly straightened the tiller to avoid colliding with the port bank and steered *Rag Albert* around the gentle left-hand bend, all the while looking for potential mooring points, as he was going to have to pull over to investigate the sudden death of the engine.

Luckily for them, they were coming in to the popular tie up by the 'Abbot's Harbour Teashop.' They coasted up against the bank and Nick dispensed with his usual pageantry, preferring just to leap on to the bank, holding the painter to make sure *Rag Albert* was not going to drift off, leaving him stranded. Three minutes later they were safely tied up and Nick was back at the control panel trying to see what the problem was. He had encountered most failures during his long love affair with the water and felt fairly sure he could resolve whatever the problem was. There were always the usual things to check first: had the diesel run out; had a fuse blown; was there a blockage? That said, Nick had never had an engine just die on him before, with no warning whatsoever.

The girls knew that this wasn't going to be resolved quickly, a brief look at his face told them that.

'I suggest we leave him to it,' said Esther as she and Boo stepped on to the towpath. 'Let's go and explore.'

There were about twenty boats all moored up

along the bank. It was a popular place if for no other reason than there was a great tearoom and a pub, the Cross Keys, both within staggering distance.

'I know,' said Sandy, 'let's go back to the bridge and see if that guy is still there,' and with that, the troupe set off down the canal path. She wasn't sure what they were going to find, but it seemed better than sitting watching Nick working on the engine.

Boo was rushing around like a coiled spring, she had been boat-bound all afternoon and was now making the most of it. There wasn't a smell that she wasn't going to savour, not a nook or cranny that she wasn't going to investigate and not a duck that she wasn't going to bark at.

Slowly, the girls coaxed her towards the arch and as they did, the strangest thing happened. Firstly, she stopped barking and she stood stock still in the middle of the path. Then, she slowly edged her way along the track, her tail drooping as she went until it was firmly planted between her legs and at that point her head was down as well. Then, she began to let out an uncharacteristic low growl.

'She can see me.'

The man stepped out of the shadows and stood before them on the path.

'Obviously,' said Esther, trying to take control. 'You can see me.'

'Sure,' added Ellen.

'And hear me.' A tear slowly rolled from the man's eye and made its way down his dirty cheek, leaving a slightly cleaner track as it went.

Boo cowered at Ellen's feet and the four of them stood in silence.

The man was dressed in thick corduroy trousers, tied with what appeared to be string just under the knees, a coarse shirt that looked a little like sack cloth, a waist coat, neckerchief and flat cap. On his feet was a pair of incredibly thickly soled boots.

'What's your name?' asked Sandy, knowing that she had to find out what was going on.

'John. John Bearchill. I have been waiting here, hoping that someone would come by that I could talk to.'

'What do you mean? There are people coming by here every day. Why haven't you spoken to them?'

'They can't see or hear me.'

The girls looked at each other. The reality – or should I say the lack of reality – was beginning to kick in.

'I need your help. I need to get a message through to someone. I need to set things right.'

'How long have you been waiting?' Sandy

asked, hoping to find out more about him.

'I was working on the canal back in 1794, when I was murdered.'

The girls were silent. They couldn't believe what they had just heard.

'I had left my wife and son to come here and work as a navvie. I didn't have any other trade and I was sending money back to them and saving everything I could. They never knew what really happened to me. They were told that I had not turned up for work one day and it was assumed I had run off with a girl from the tavern. I couldn't leave it like that – I had to find someone who could explain to my family what really happened, someone that could help me put the record straight.'

'Have you any idea what year it is?' asked Ellen, fighting with the thought that this all had to be a dream.

'No. I just know I have been waiting a long time.'

'Your family will be long dead,' said Esther, trying not to sound too harsh. 'Not only them, but their children and their children's children. In fact, I don't know how many generations will have come and gone while you've been waiting.'

The man stood quietly before speaking again. 'I was afraid of that, but somehow I need to have my story told before I can pass over and find my wife and child.'

'How can we help?' said Sandy, beginning to feel that this was an opportunity to make a difference, even though the circumstances were rather unbelievable.

'As soon as you waved to me, I knew my wait was over. That's why I stopped your engine. I had been waiting for someone sensitive enough to be able to communicate with me and now you are here. I was murdered because I loved my family. I saved every halfpenny I earned so that I could send it back to Sarah, and that was my undoing. Richard Pinkerton, one of the navvies in my gang, had run up gambling debts and owed a lot of money to the tavern. He knew that if he didn't pay them off he was going to be found floating in the canal, so he took what he thought was the easy option. He knew that I had cash, probably enough cash to clear what he owed, so he waited until after we had all gone to sleep and then he slipped into my tent and throttled me with my own necker-chief. I tried to struggle, but he was stronger than me. I tried to call out, but I found no voice. Then I remember looking down at him riffling through my pack and taking my money.'

The girls listened intently, absolutely transfixed by what he was saying, almost forgetting that they were standing there talking to a ghost.

'Then what happened?'

'He then carried my body out from the tent and brought it here, to where we were building the bridge. That is why I am here now – I am part of the foundations. He tipped my body in behind the retaining wall and then covered me with rubble.'

Sandy looked at him. Her face was wracked with sadness at the man's story. She could feel tears welling up in her eyes, but she knew she had to be strong.

'Tell me what we can do.'

'Take my wedding ring as proof and tell people where I am. Make sure that my descendants know that I didn't run off. Tell them that I loved my family to the end. Tell them not to think badly of me.'

It was a simple request.

'And if we do, will you be able to move on?'

'That is all I need.'

Chapter 9

Boo walked forward quietly and sat at John's feet. She leant against his leg and looked up soulfully, or at least as soulfully as a terrier can. John looked down and smiled.

Sandy stepped forward, a newly found confidence driving her on.

'Tell me exactly what we need to do,' she said with an air of determination even she herself didn't recognise. 'Where is your ring?'

John stretched out his arm. He unclenched his hand and extended his ring finger.

'There.'

She moved towards him and made to take his hand.

'No,' he said firmly but not unkindly, 'it is on my real finger. You will find me behind the wall.'

Sandy turned to look at the bridge. Her gaze followed the path of his extended finger, which seemed to be pointing at a large square rock set into the wall about two feet off the towpath.

Not sure what she was now supposed to do, she moved towards the rock, closely followed by the two girls. Boo remained at his feet, as if trying to offer some comfort after so many solitary years.

'I need you to hold the picture of my hand and the ring firmly in your mind and then to reach forward.'

Sandy did exactly that. She half closed her eyes and visualised the ring she had seen on the ghost's finger. She then reached forward and waited for her fingernails to rub up against the coarse surface of the stone. It didn't.

'Now that is cool! No one at school is going to believe this.'

Esther's outburst, after having been quiet for so long, took Sandy by surprise and it momentarily broke her concentration. She opened her eyes and saw that the fingers of her hand appeared to be inside the rock. She instinctively withdrew her hand, almost as if she had been burned.

'Will you just shut up?' barked Ellen, realising what had happened.

'Sorry.'

'Try again,' said John reassuringly. 'You were

doing really well.'

Once again, Sandy half closed her eyes and pictured the band on his finger. She stretched forward, meeting no resistance and this time she reached in further than before. Her whole hand had now disappeared into the rock.

'What now?'

John spoke calmly and quietly.

'Move your hand around as if you are trying to find a walnut in a sack of flour.'

Now this wasn't an analogy that she was used to, but under the circumstances she knew exactly what he meant. She began to rummage around, not really knowing what to expect and trying not to be put off by the fact that her arm now seemed to stop halfway to her elbow.

'Remember,' he said, 'you are trying to find me.'

Sandy felt a wave of nausea roll over her. It was stupid she knew, but somewhere just in front of her was a body. Not just any body, but the body of a man she felt she knew, a man standing not five feet away from her.

She tried to tell herself that this was no different from the journey through the graveyard at Gill Church that she and Ellen had taken earlier that day. There were bodies all around them then, but this felt different. It was different. The bodies in the cemetery had had a decent burial. They had had a proper funeral with mourners and hymns. They had had an official send off by a vicar and their families had been there to say goodbye.

In front of her now was the body of a man who had met an untimely and unjust end and whose family never had closure. They had been left with only an assumption of his demise and who had never had a chance to say farewell.

The nausea drained away and was replaced by a feeling of anger. Anger for the way that this man had been treated. Anger for the injustice of the whole situation and anger that a guilty man had got away with murder.

'I feel something,' she suddenly exclaimed. 'It feels like rough material rather than smooth rock.'

'Probably my shirt,' John replied. 'Feel around until you find my sleeve. Focus, picture it in your mind.'

Sandy did exactly that and soon she found her hand running down the length of his arm, finding the thicker material of his cuff.

Without warning she let out a shriek and again she pulled her arm back out from the bridge.

Ellen and Esther stood there transfixed. It looked like someone wafting their arm through thick smoke. Her arm, or the rock – or perhaps both – billowed and swirled and then snapped back into place as if nothing had happened.

'I think, I think I just felt ...'

'The bones of my hand,' John finished the sentence for her.

'I'm so sorry,' babbled Sandy apologetically. 'I knew what to expect but I've never touched a skeleton before.'

John smiled.

'Nor have I,' he quipped, making Sandy feel like she wasn't such a fool after all. 'At least you know where my hand is now and what to expect next time,' he said, putting her totally at ease.

Sandy felt Ellen's hand on her shoulder.

'Go on. You can do it. You have done amazingly so far.'

She felt the warmth of pride, something she had not felt much of in her short life, and it felt good. She stepped back towards the bridge and without closing her eyes this time, she thrust her arm back in to where she had felt John's bony fingers.

'I can feel your hand.'

'Excellent. Now I want you to focus really hard on the ring. You need to be able to see it in as much detail as possible' and with that he raised his hand up in front of Sandy's face so that she could see the ghostly representation of what was buried in front of her.

'I've got it!' she exclaimed triumphantly. 'I can

feel it with my fingers.'

'Now,' said John, 'here's the hard part. I want you to take all that anger, all that emotion that you were just feeling, and hold it tight in your heart. Then I want you to close your hand around the ring and pull it out, holding it tight, so tight that it's squashed into your palm.'

Sandy did exactly as she was told. Tears welled up as she channelled the anger and emotion. She threw in how Miss Simpson had made her feel earlier, just to add to the pot, and how annoyed she had felt at the trial when the other girls had stopped her from showing just how good she was.

'Here it is!'

Sandy was standing absolutely still, she had her other hand wrapped around the closed fist, both so tightly squeezed that the whites of her knuckles were clearly visible.

'Great job!' cheered Esther. 'Let's see what you've got.'

Esther, Ellen and John all moved forward as Sandy raised her left hand and slowly unfurled her fingers to show a dull metal band lying in the centre of her palm, slightly sunk into a dent she had put there by how tightly she had been holding the object. There was no way she was going to let this accidentally slip out of her grasp.

'Now pick it up and see what is written inside.'

The light was beginning to fade, but it was still bright enough to read by. Sandy tilted the band so that she could see what was inscribed on the inside.

'John and Sarah forever.'

'I scratched that myself,' said John proudly. 'Did the same on Sarah's, too.'

It was a simple message, but a heartfelt one from an equally simple navvie to his bride. It had now been passed to Sandy and she willingly accepted what she now had to do.

'I will make sure that this gets to the right person,' she promised John. She had never been so determined about anything else before in her life.

'Then there is nothing more that can be done here,' he said with a look of relief and expectation on his face. 'I must wait here until you have found that person, then I can leave.'

'Let's get back to the boat.'

The girls made their farewells and set off briskly back down the towpath. Boo stayed behind briefly, but then barked once and padded off to follow them.

As they neared the boat they could just see Nick's rear end sticking out of the engine compartment.

'I have absolutely no idea what the problem is,' he said with a sigh of exasperation.

'I shouldn't worry too much about it,' said Sandy as she climbed back aboard the boat. 'I have a feeling it's going to start now.'

Nick closed the hatch and made his way back to the stern. He reached for the ignition that had given him so much trouble and resolutely turned it one more time.

The engine sprang to life. Not only did it spring to life, but it sounded smoother than it had done for years.

'Well, I'll be ...' said Nick.

The girls, now all sitting once again on the roof, looked at one another and nodded. They had a secret, something that probably no one else could understand and one that they felt they could not yet share with Nick.

'All hands on deck and belay the bow rope,' came the comforting cry from Nick. It was a blast of normality following the strange events of the last hour or so.

With the engine barely ticking over, he expertly turned the boat without hitting the bank and set off back the way they had come.

'It'll be dark by the time we get home,' he said, as he switched on the night lights so as to make himself more visible in the twilight of that summer evening.

As they motored carefully back under the bridge,

four pairs of eyes were searching for the outline of John. As if on cue, a figure stepped forward and this time, with a beaming smile, he waved at the girls. They frantically responded and Sandy held up her hand, her fist holding on to the ring for dear life, so as to send him a message of hope. John placed his hand over his heart and then pointed back at Sandy, his meaning clear to all. He turned and seemed to disappear into the dark green ivy that clung to the stonework like a blanket, just as a young family cycled through together, their laughter somehow incongruous with the surroundings.

'If only they knew,' thought Sandy, pressing the ring even harder in to her palm.

She sat back down, her mind racing, but strangely at peace. Her thoughts now turned to the task at hand. How on earth was she going to trace John's ancestors? She had no idea where to start. Were they likely to be local, given that Sarah had stayed behind when John came to work here? Had he mentioned where he had come from? Sandy wracked her brain; no, she was fairly sure he had never said where his family was. She wished now that she had asked him, but it was too late. She couldn't really ask Nick to turn the boat around again, besides, they would have to explain every-thing to him and for the moment they were going to keep him out of it. She could probably use the internet in the IT room at school on Monday. Seemed most of the kids spent half their life on the web and for once it could be put to good use rather than just talking to friends that were probably sat at the next computer.

'What was it like?'

Sandy turned to look at Esther.

'What was it like when you put your hand in to the rock? It looked so cool!'

'Difficult to describe, really,' replied Sandy, trying to find the right words. 'To start with, there was a sort of passive resistance, like putting your hand into water I suppose, but without it being wet. It wasn't dry dry, like pushing your hand in to flour, but it wasn't like a liquid. Does that make sense?'

'Not really, but to be honest nothing much has since I got up this morning,' said Esther, feeling like she had been a bystander watching the last 24 hours go by rather than being a normal person taking part in a normal day.

By now the earlier twilight had given way to dusk and the green and red lights on either side of the boat were glowing like Christmas decorations. Nick had also turned on the white steaming light at the front and the white stern light at the back, turning off all other lights so as not to blind or distract him. It was dangerous travelling at night and all the crew had to look out to ensure they did not hit the bank or – worse still – another boat. Having said that, they had not seen any other traffic on the canal for nearly 20 minutes as most boats had moored up once darkness approached. It is not an easy job steering a boat some 60 feet long and 6 feet ten inches wide while standing right at the back, but Nick was a professional and although the journey back was taking longer than the outward trek, due to the need for slower speed in the dark, their progress was steady.

Ahead of them, a lock was coming into view and Sandy could feel a knot forming in her stomach. She had found the first lock quite scary and that was in the light. This was going to be an entirely different proposition. She looked back at Nick, breathing a sigh of relief to see he was already wearing a lifebelt. It was a dry night which helped, because any moisture could make the inevitable walk across the bridge quite tortuous. In fact, the majority of lock keepers wouldn't let boats through at night due to the increased risk of accidents. One slip and you could be thrown into not only cold, but turbulent water, if the paddles have already been opened.

She needn't have worried.

In his usual, capable style Nick went through his

traditional mooring routine and then set about working the lock. Courtesy dictates that you always check to see if there is a boat likely to be entering the head gate on the upper level of the canal before entering from the lower. This is not only polite, but stops the waste of water that comes with the unnecessary use of the locks. After all, a canal needs to be topped up from a reservoir to keep it running.

After a brief check, Nick, armed with his trusty windlass, began the age-old sequence of events that hadn't changed since John and his fellow navvies had first dug the canal. The rushing water seemed eerie in the darkness and the three girls never took their eyes off Nick as he clambered about the lock, making sure that he never lost his footing.

The boat began to rise and the familiar bumping of the gunwale against the inner wall of the lock reassured them that everything was going smoothly. It also informed them that they were not too far from home now.

Chapter 10

As the girls saw the familiar site of the gate keeper's cottage at Greenberfield pass by, they knew they were on the final leg of their eventful journey.

The town houses of the estate built high above them on their left signalled their approach in to Barlick. Warm, comforting light escaped from around the edges of curtains drawn against the chilling night air and there was the flicker of citronella candles burning in a back garden where people were standing around the embers of a late barbeque. The smell of previously cooked sausages and burgers wafted down to the boat and Sandy realised that she hadn't actually eaten anything that day.

'Now that smells good,' exclaimed Nick, catching the aroma fractionally later than the girls, being positioned on the stern of the boat.

Faces appeared at the back fence of the garden and they looked down, waving, not used to seeing boats moving on the water this late at night. The girls waved back and Nick gave a quick salute as the engine took them ever closer to home with each methodical firing of the cylinders.

'Shame they didn't throw down a hotdog,' quipped Nick, trying to stay focused on the task at hand.

Under the Skipton Road and then past the Coates Estate, the terrain more than familiar now.

'Still got the ring?' asked Ellen, somewhat redundantly as you would have had to cut Sandy's hand off to get her to part with it.

'You betcha!' came the reply although Sandy did open her fingers to peek in just to make sure. The gentle pain in her hand already confirmed that not only did she still have it, but that she was holding it too tightly, but never-the-less she still wanted to check. This was too important an item to let it slip into the canal at this point.

When they saw Long Ing Lane pass over head, they realised that it would be only a few more minutes. The bed factory was lit up and a few nightshift workers could be heard singing as they moved about, loading beds on to trucks with their forklifts. The security lamps cast dancing shadows on the water as the reeds swayed in the night time breeze and the surface of the canal rippled from the movement of the boat. As they motored beyond the industrious workers, their laughter and shouting was replaced by the strident call of the reed warblers that inhabited the undergrowth. 'Pretty to listen to, but you wouldn't want one living outside your bedroom window,' thought Sandy.

Nick throttled down even more than he already had as they approached Lower Park Marina. He knew that a boat going through at this late hour would provoke a response from his fellow boaters and give them something to talk about tomorrow as they supped their breakfast coffees and put the world to rights. He was not disappointed, as no sooner had the bow passed the first boat than curtains were slid along and faces pressed against the windows. He maintained a stoic indifference, deciding that this was better than waving, which might be seen as rubbing salt in the wound as he felt sure he had woken some people up. If anyone took issue in the morning he could always simply apologise and regale the story of the unexplained engine failure.

Cockshott Bridge, now Kelbrook Road Bridge and then there was home. The twinkling of the lights from the Anchor through the leaves on the trees signalled their arrival.

While Nick secured the mooring ropes, Sandy, Esther, Ellen and Boo all jumped off the boat.

'Some day, huh?'

'I'd better get back,' said Sandy, hugging Ellen and then Esther. 'They will probably have reported me as missing. I'll be back first thing and then we can decide what we do next.'

With a thoughtful pat of Boo's head, Sandy turned and left the others as shadows on the towpath. This had been a truly strange and magical day, but despite being worn out, both emotionally and physically, she knew she was unlikely to sleep tonight.

Chapter 11

Saturday morning began the way that Saturdays should. A big yolk of a sun began to push its head above the moorland behind Kelbrook and the golden glow that it sent forth made the heather look as if it was on fire. Wisps of mist floated in the valley along to Foulridge, but they were quickly being burned off as they lost the battle with the rising temperature.

In the distance was the cackle of a grouse, spooked by the late return of a hunting fox and the general hum of a million insects filled the air like audible wallpaper.

Along the towpath the ducks began to stretch their legs, sifting through the grass to see if they could find anything worth eating that had been left by the tourists and fishermen. A couple of field mice scuttled for cover, trying to avoid becoming breakfast for the kestrel, soaring lazily above on young thermals that were warming themselves and growing in strength as the sun made its way higher in the sky.

It had to be said it was about as close to being perfect as you could ever get in Salterforth. Oh yes, there was one other creature already up and perched on the bridge. Correct ... it was Sandy.

She couldn't remember the whole of last night, so she assumed she had managed to grab some sleep, but she was up, raring to go and was a woman on a mission. She knew she shouldn't go and wake the boat. Nick, for one, probably needed his rest after an unusually busy and frustrating day yesterday. She had no idea about the girls, but she felt fairly sure that they would be up early as well.

She had had a fitful night and could remember visions of John standing there in front of her, holding out his hand with the ring missing. She had woken with a start and immediately checked to see that the ring was still there, exactly where she had left it when she went to bed, in her hand! Her palm was bruised now, but she didn't care. All she wanted was to see the girls coming off the boat and then for them to hold a council of war to decide what to do next. To her great relief, she was about to get her wish.

'Get off!' came a familiar shout. 'I bet she's waiting for us.' Esther's distinctive tone cut through the early morning quiet like a hot knife through butter.

'She's probably still in bed, if she's got any sense, like I would be if I didn't have the dubious pleasure of sharing a room with you.' Ellen's protestations fell on deaf ears. 'I'll swear you have an internal alarm clock that is set to go off at whatever time is going to hack me off the most!'

Sandy could hear the argument all the way down to the bridge and felt fairly sure that all the boaters that were moored up by the Anchor would now probably be awake too. She grinned broadly – they were great value for money these two and Boo was just the icing on the cake. The dog was now joining in, with Ellen desperately trying to get her to stop barking and Esther, unfazed by it all, was just breathing in the clear morning air, preparing herself for whatever life was going to throw at her that weekend. Friends like this were hard to find.

Sandy scooted down off the wall where she had been sitting, somewhat precariously, with her legs dangling over the canal. She had been there for nearly an hour and, apart from the pins and needles in her feet and the fact that her bum had gone numb, she felt quite elated. She wasn't quite sure how to proceed from here, but she had an important promise to fulfil and she was going to honour that commitment come hell or high water.

She skipped down the path until the girls looked up, waved and started along the track to meet her. None of them was quite sure what to say or where to begin, so they began the day with a group hug.

'That was a day for the diary!' said Esther, stating the obvious but at least breaking the silence, and then everyone began to talk at once.

After about five minutes of the three of them speaking and not one of them listening, they all went quiet again, if for no other reason than they needed to breath. At that point Sandy looked up and saw the familiar figure of Val jogging towards them with Matthew, as always, sat in his buggy. Val hadn't seen them yet and as Sandy knew, there was no point shouting as she always had her iPod blasting away through her earphones.

'It's Val,' she said to Esther and Ellen as she pointed towards her friend. 'Perhaps she'll know what to do.'

'It's a long shot,' thought Sandy, but she had always found Val easy to talk to and felt that the two of them had some kind of connection. She decided she would stop and talk to her when she reached their merry band.

Then, from nowhere, a mink came careening out of the undergrowth, making a mad dash for the canal. It obviously didn't look before breaking cover because it ran right in between Val and her buggy. She never saw it at all and in her oblivious state she tripped and fell forward. She lost control of the buggy and while Sandy watched in horror, the mink dived into the water, closely followed by Matthew still strapped into the buggy. It all seemed to be happening in slow motion and then Val, desperately trying to regain control, threw herself towards the canal in an effort to grab Matthew. Because she had been off balance, instead of being able to grab the buggy before it hurtled over the edge of the bank, Val's rescue attempt ended with a gut-wrenching dull thud as her face collided with the hull of *Rag Albert*. The girls froze, but only for a second and then they all moved as one.

Sandy ran towards Val, who was not moving at all and there was blood trickling down her face from a nasty looking gash on her forehead. Esther and Ellen rushed towards the boat and with their feet hardly touching the deck, they hurled themselves into the water, closely followed by Boo.

Sandy cradled Val, who was now coming to.

'Where's Matthew, where's my baby!' she screamed, trying to wipe the blood from her eyes so she could see what was happening.

'Don't worry,' said Sandy, realising, as she was saying it, that it was probably the most stupid thing she could have said under the circumstances, 'the girls will get him.'

Esther's head appeared first. However, she gulped in air and then dipped down under the water again.

'Oh my God, where are they?' cried Val, completely unaware that she not only had a cut on her head, but also that her nose was quite obviously broken.

Just as she finished speaking, Ellen and Esther broke surface at the same time, holding on to the buggy for grim death. They made their way to the bank and Val and Sandy leaned forward to grab it and haul it on to the towpath.

'Thank you, oh, thank you!' sobbed Val and then she suddenly let out a blood curdling yell. 'Where's Matthew, he's not here!'

The straps were open and where he should have been sitting was just a soaking wet blanket that had been wrapped around him to keep him warm against the early morning chill.

Esther and Ellen hurled themselves backwards, ready to dive below the murky water and nearly collided with Boo, who was swimming towards them with Matthew's sweatshirt held firmly in her teeth. Thankfully Matthew was still wearing it and although a little bemused, he seemed to be in good health. Everybody grabbed him at the same time and Val hugged him so tightly to her chest that the girls were worried he might be squashed. Somewhat ironic to be crushed to death after surviving a possible drowning!

'What the hell is all the noise about?'

Nick appeared on deck, obviously having been awoken by all the commotion, not to mention the incredible thud of Val's face hitting the boat.

Nobody spoke, but Nick looked down at Val and suddenly realised the gravity of the situation.

'Oh my God, what's happened? Let me help you,' and he sprang off the boat, putting his arms around Val and Matthew together. 'Come aboard and sit down.'

Nick steered them on to the boat and into the galley. He grabbed a throw rug and wrapped it around the pair of them. He then ripped half a dozen sheets of paper off the kitchen roll and first wiped Val's face before holding them against the gash just below her hairline.

'Is the boy OK? Are you OK? Are you hurt anywhere else?'

The questions came thick and fast as Nick took complete control of the situation. Val choked out answers, but they were difficult to hear as she was talking with her face buried in Matthew's neck. To be honest, he seemed completely unaware of the near-death experience and he was looking from face to face trying to find the dog. The three girls had climbed inside by now. Sandy had slid on to the same bench that Val was on and Esther and Ellen were sitting on the step with Boo at their feet. They were looking terrified and relieved all at once and the water was dripping off them on to the floor.

'Are you OK?' shouted Nick, trying to get a definite answer from an obviously traumatised Val.

'I'm fine, we're fine,' she replied, shaken back into reality through Nick's sharp words. 'Nothing broken, apart from possibly my nose,' she said, as the pain suddenly became intense following the initial surge of adrenaline. She raised her hand to her face and winced. She took the paper towel from Nick and pressed it painfully against her forehead. Nick slumped back into the cushion.

'What on earth happened?' he asked, trying to make some sense out of the bleeding woman and the soaking child.

Val set to and explained everything that had taken place right up to the point where Nick appeared. How she had tripped, how she had hit the boat and how Matthew had been rescued by his daughters.

'Are you sure you feel all right?' he asked leaning forward to check for other head wounds.

'Sure,' came the reply, her heartbeat now having returned to almost normal. 'Apart from the cut and the nose, I think I'm fine and Matthew seems to not even have a scratch.'

Nick looked at her somewhat aghast. 'You see,' he said slowly, 'I don't have any kids.'

Chapter 12

Val looked at Sandy and then they both looked at Nick.

'I don't follow you,' said Val, somewhat lost for words.

'Fairly simple,' said Nick, 'My wife died a long time ago and we never had any kids. You are probably just not remembering things properly because of the bang on the head. Don't worry about it. I think I'd better call you an ambulance.'

Nick made to stand up but Val started to talk again so he sat back down.

'I was with them when I waved to you on a number of occasions when I was out jogging.'

'Oh, you're the lady who has been waving. Sorry,

I hadn't put two and two together. I never really got a good look at your face. There are lots of people who wave when you live on a boat. Didn't see any kids with you, but as I said, didn't really pay much attention.'

'Esther and Ellen,' said Val slowly, her voice beginning to crack a little.

Nick's face seemed to pale and he leant forward in his seat.

'I have lived on this boat for going on fifteen years, sadly ten of those on my own. I bought the boat off Stan Gillingworth, who had owned it from new. Stan decided to move back to dry land after the tragic loss of his daughters who fell through the ice in the bad winter about sixteen years ago. They had foolishly been trying to rescue their dog that had wandered out on to the canal, thinking it was safe to walk on. They were called Esther and Ellen.'

Silence fell around the table. Val turned and looked at Sandy. Neither spoke. Neither could speak.

'You must be mixing up what happened today with something you have heard about that terrible accident. Happens all the time with bangs to the head. I'll go and call the ambulance. The Anchor will let me use their phone, I don't have a mobile.' And with that he walked up the step, across the deck and on to the towpath.

Val and Sandy both turned to look at the step

where the girls had been sitting. There were two damp semicircles on the first step and two pools of water on the floor. Just to the side of the puddles were four small paw prints, perfectly outlined in water and behind them the outline of a tail.

Outside on the bank, Esther, Ellen and Boo were talking to a tall, beautiful woman.

'You have done a wonderful thing here today,' she said, putting her hands on the girls' shoulders, 'and you too, Boo.' Boo barked. 'You may not have been able to save yourselves or your dog all those years ago, but you have now saved the boy, and his mother will always be grateful. Now run along and say that Margret Rose Pendle sent you.'

The girls walked off down the towpath towards The Anchor. 'I will say goodbye to Sandy for you.'

They ducked under the bridge, but never came out the other side.

Back on the boat Sandy and Val were trying to come to terms with what had just happened. 'But I've seen you all together,' exclaimed Val, struggling with the implications of what Nick had said.

'I've spent the last week with them,' said Sandy, still reeling from what had happened yesterday, never mind trying to assimilate what had just happened this morning.

After a moment's quiet, Sandy spoke.

'This may not be the right time to bring this

up,' she began slowly, but determinedly, 'but there is something I need to tell you and somehow this seems like the right moment.'

Val sat there, listening to every detail. Her head was hurting from the blow, but what Sandy was now saying made her head hurt even more.

'So, you are telling me that you think this man was a ghost and that Ellen and Esther are ghosts too?' She was struggling to get her head around it all. In fact, had she not just gone through the previous half an hour, she would have dismissed Sandy's story as the over imaginative mind of a teenage girl.

'Yes,' said Sandy, trying to look confident, having just explained what must have been the most unexplainable set of events ever.

'And I promised John that I would help to clear his name, but I have no idea how to do it. All I have is this ring.' With that, Sandy thrust her hand into her pocket and pulled out the ring that she had retrieved from the bridge the previous day. She leaned forward and laid it in front of Val.

'All he wants is for someone to remove his body from the bridge and to give him a proper burial. That, and to tell his family what really happened.'

Val looked at the ring for what seemed like minutes without uttering a single word. Sandy wondered if the shock of the injury was now starting to kick in.

'Are you feeling OK?' she asked, concerned that Val was going to pass out and drop Matthew.

Val looked up, her eyes misting over. Without saying a word she let go of Matthew for a moment and reached behind her own neck. She unclasped her necklace and let it slip into an uneven pile of chain on the table top where Sandy could see it. Sandy's eyes focused on what the chain was carrying; a ring. She picked it up and looked inside. There was an inscription.

'Sarah and John forever.'

Sandy couldn't believe it. All she could do was blurt out 'But, but ...'

'My father's name was Bearchill. My name was Bearchill until I got married. John was my great-great-grandfather. This ring has been handed down from my great-great-grandmother who always told the story of how her husband went missing, but she never believed the story of his disappearance. It was always passed on with the promise expected that whoever had the ring was to try and solve the mystery of John's disappearance. I always thought it was just a story.'

Val was rolling John's wedding ring in her fingers and Sandy was doing the same with Sarah's.

'I guess you know the truth now.'

By the double-arch bridge at Marton, John turned

to look at the stone that he had shown to Sandy the day before. He smiled. His wife's arms were held out towards him and he could hear his son's laughter. He walked forward and into the bridge. A golden haze momentarily lit the shadows under the over-hanging trees and then he was gone.

Back on the boat, Val and Sandy could hear Nick coming back from the pub.

'They say the ambulance will be here in about 10 minutes,' he explained as he sat back down opposite her. 'How are you feeling? It looks like you have stopped bleeding but that nose looks awfully sore. Is your head feeling any clearer now?'

Val thought for a minute and then replied with a simple 'Yes.' There seemed little point in taking this any further with Nick. She needed time to think.

'I did remember one thing,' he said in a matter of fact manner as he reached for the kettle. 'You know I said that the two girls had drowned trying to save their dog? Well, that wasn't the end of the story. There was a third girl, can't remember her name. She apparently had just moved into the area, no one knew her really, but she saw what was happening and tried to help. God love her, the water was only five feet or so deep, but it was so cold you see, she didn't stand a chance.'

Val froze, as if ice was running through her veins. How much more could she take in one day?

Sandy had vanished.

***

By the bridge stood Margaret Rose Pendle. She was slowly explaining to Sandy that she had, in fact, died all those years ago when she fell through the ice. Because she hadn't realised this, she had been re-living the same year over and over again. That was why no one had been able to see her until this year when she had met Val, whose story was interwoven with her own.

Sandy thought for a moment. It explained why she had only been able to move the netball or to tie the bow rope when her emotions were running wild. Why she had been able to walk into Gill Church despite the two closed doors.

Suddenly it all became clear. She, too, was a ghost.

'You wanted to make friends this year,' she said, almost in a whisper, 'and you have made the best friends you could ever have. Such a friendship will last forever. You should feel very proud of yourself. Now go and join the girls, they are waiting for you.'

Sandy looked under the arch where Margaret was pointing. She smiled.

'Just give her a minute will you?' The unmistakable sound of Ellen trying to reason with Esther. 'At least let them finish their conversation.'

With a peal of laughter Sandy ran under the bridge and a flash of light heralded their departure.

Chapter 13

A lthough it was a terrible day, weatherwise, the turn out at the church was impressive. The rain had lashed down all morning and the wind had been blowing a gale.

Although Val had decided to keep the story of what had happened private, she had not been able to hide everything, particularly as it had entailed the partial dismantling of the double-arch bridge at Marton. The police had been involved, the forensics team, the local council, British Waterways, in fact it had turned in to a circus. Despite this, Val had remained calm. She had been through so much since that fateful day when she nearly lost her son – enough to make her think that nothing would ever be able to faze her again.

Just as the coffin was carried out towards the freshly dug grave, the rain stopped, as did the wind.

Val smiled. 'Divine intervention,' she thought to herself as she squeezed Matthew's hand.

While the vicar was waxing lyrical by the graveside, as vicars do, Val watched the coffin of John Bearchill being slowly lowered into the grave.

'You have done a wonderful thing here today.'

Val turned to look at the woman standing next to her. 'I'm sorry, do I know you?'

'Margret Rose Pendle.' She put her hand out and touched Val's arm.

'My friends call me Midnight Rose. There are some people who want to say hello.' With that she pointed back towards the entrance of the church.

Standing in front of the old oak door were the girls waving madly. Boo was barking and Ellen was trying to get Esther to shut up as she was whistling loudly, quite inappropriately considering where they were and what was happening.

Val laughed out loud and the other mourners looked disapprovingly at her.

'Look Mummy,' said Matthew as he waved back towards the church.

'I see them,' said Val. She picked him up so that he could get a better view and then the girls walked back into the church, still pushing and shoving each other as they went.

She turned to thank Margaret, but she was no longer there.